the DOUGHNUT FIX

JESSIE JANOWITZ

sourcebooks jabberwocky

Published by Sourcebooks Jabberwocky, an imprint of Sourcebooks, Inc.
P.O. Box 4410, Naperville, Illinois 60567-4410
(630) 961-3900
Fax: (630) 961-2168
sourcebooks.com

Library of Congress Cataloging-in-Publication Data

Names: Janowitz, Jessie, author.
Title: The doughnut fix / Jessie Janowitz.
Description: Naperville, Illinois : Sourcebooks Jabberwocky, [2018] | Series: The doughnut fix ; 1 | Summary: When his family moves to tiny Petersville, eleven-year-old Tris stops focusing on his perfect sister, Jeanine, by using his cooking expertise to revive a town tradition of chocolate cream doughnuts.
Identifiers: LCCN 2017034429 | (13 : alk. paper)
Subjects: | CYAC: Family life--Fiction. | Community life--Fiction. | Doughnuts--Fiction. | Moving, Household--Fiction.
Classification: LCC PZ7.1.J3882 Dou 2018 | DDC [Fic]--dc23 LC record available at https://lccn.loc.gov/2017034429

Source of Production: Berryville Graphics, Inc. Berryville, Virginia, USA
Date of Production: February 2018
Run Number: 5011523

Printed and bound in the United States of America.
BVG 10 9 8 7 6 5 4 3 2 1

For Toby, Leo, and Sylvie

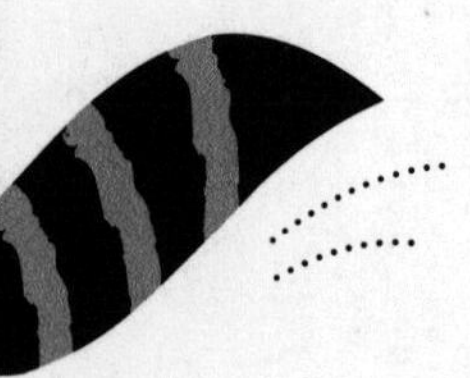

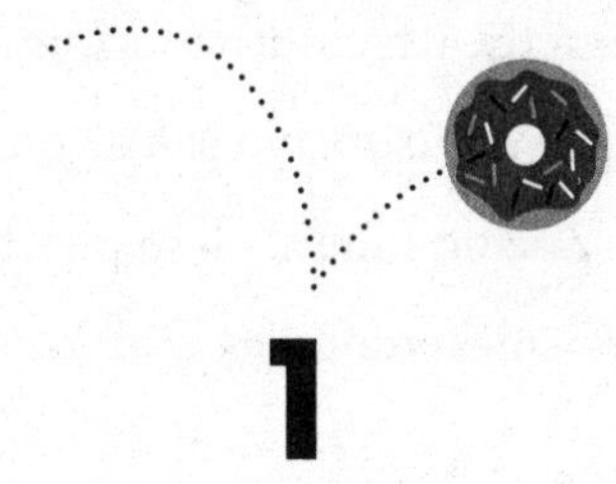

1

It started off like any normal Saturday with Jeanine, Zoe, and me flipping through cookbooks on the living room floor.

For Mom, teaching us to bake was right up there with teaching us to read. As soon as we were old enough to digest chocolate, we got a Dessert Day, one day a week to make whatever we wanted. We'd pick our recipes on Saturday morning, then shop for ingredients after eating breakfast at Barney Greengrass, a deli a few blocks up Amsterdam Avenue from our apartment.

I'd been working my way through *Roland Mesnier's Basic to Beautiful Cakes* since I got it for my birthday in July. Roland is king when it comes to cake. He was the White House pastry chef for twenty-five years.

That morning, I decided to tackle the white chocolate dome

cake Roland created for President Jimmy Carter, minus the nasty orange syrup he uses. Except for cutting out stuff I hate, I usually follow the recipe exactly, which drives Mom crazy. She says you have to make a recipe your own, but she's a professional.

As usual, it took Zoe no time at all to pick her dessert, because she always chooses snickerdoodles and knows the ingredients by heart.

Jeanine couldn't make up her mind between triple chocolate chip cookies and banoffee pie. Jeanine is Gifted and Talented, which means no matter the question, she's always sure there's a right answer. So when there is no right or wrong, when it's just red or blue, plain or sesame, she totally falls apart.

I was rooting for the cookies for the simple reason that banoffee pie is disgusting. It never even gets cooked, so it's all cold and slimy like hand sanitizer. I kept my opinion to myself though. I may be two years older, but Jeanine never listens to me about anything, not even dessert.

According to the New York City Department of Education, I, Tristan Levin, am not Gifted or Talented. I can make a perfect chocolate chip cookie, but Mom made sure we could all do that. I'm not entirely clear on what about me isn't G&T material, but I'm guessing the fact that I still use my fingers to do the nines trick has something to do with it. When Jeanine turned seven, it was like God had downloaded every single multiplication fact right into her brain.

What I do get about the whole G&T thing is that it's not something I can change. I'm pretty good at knowing what I can control and what I can't. I guess that's not something G&T tests for because Jeanine never knows.

I used to think my name was one of those things that I was just stuck with, but then I found out you can legally change your own name. Charlie's Uncle Ralph, now Uncle Damien, did it. Personally, I don't think Damien's any better than Ralph, but neither are as bad as Tristan.

What do you think of Jax? There's something especially cool about a name with an *X* in it, right? But then, sometimes I wonder if it sounds too much like a dog: "Here, Jax! Roll over, Jax!" You can't change your name till you're eighteen, and I'm only twelve, so I've got some time.

When half an hour had gone by and Jeanine still hadn't picked her dessert, I told my parents I'd meet them at breakfast. Barney's opens at eight thirty, and if you're not there by nine, you'll never get a table, even if you are a regular.

Barney's isn't fancy or anything. The wallpaper is peeling and has food smears on it, and most of the chairs are crisscrossed with duct tape. But I'm telling you, none of that matters once you taste the food. If I could eat only one thing for the rest of my life, it would be Barney's eggs and onions. The eggs are so creamy, they taste like custard, and the onions are so sweet, you'd swear they were cooked in maple syrup.

Then there's the smell. Just one whiff of that air dripping with chicken soup, sautéed onions, and garlic bagels, and *Shazzam*! The whole world goes all Willy-Wonka-big-glass-elevator-crashing-through-the-ceiling happy endings. That math test I have Monday? Who cares. That gang of weight-lifting private school jerks taking over the basketball courts? No problem. It's all gonna work out just fine.

Not! That's the Barney's magic. And once you feel it, you can never get enough.

My grandmother puts up these fresh air things all over her apartment. They have names like Irish Meadow and Seaside. I want a gizmo I can plug in and *Wham*! My room smells like Barney Greengrass.

Normally, Barney's won't let you sit unless everyone in your party is there, but since we're regulars, Zippo let me go straight to our table.

"Hey, kid," he said, holding out his palm.

"Hey," I said, smacking it as I slid into a booth next to the window display of challah breads.

"The usual?" he asked, rolling a toothpick from one side of his mouth to the other.

"Uh-huh."

"What about Mom? I have to check if the kreplach's ready."

Zippo has known Mom all her life. She grew up coming to Barney's with her parents, and Zippo was already a waiter back then. The guys in the kitchen love her because she gets the kreplach. According to Zippo, very few people order kreplach anymore, and nobody but her ever orders it for breakfast, so she's something of a celebrity. If you don't know, kreplach is like Jewish wonton soup. I'm not a huge fan, but you should decide for yourself.

"She and Dad both want kreplach," I said.

"Really? Tom's getting kreplach," Zippo said, impressed. "And what about Thing One and Thing Two?"

"Plain bagels with cream cheese."

"That's it?"

"That's it," I said.

Zippo rolled his eyes and then disappeared into the kitchen.

I don't know how long I was waiting, but by the time everybody else got there, the food was already on the table, and I was halfway done. When I looked up from my plate, they were making their way through the crowd by the counter. Zoe was crying, and my father was carrying her way out in front of him to keep from getting stuck with one of the many chopsticks poking out of her hair.

Mom puts her own hair up with chopsticks when she's cooking, but she uses only two. Her hair wouldn't even hold more than two, but Zoe's hair is like Velcro—curly, orange, gravity-defying Velcro. Of course, my parents love it because the rest of us, including them, have boring, dirt-colored hair. It's not just my parents either. Everyone loves Zoe's hair: teachers, waiters, bus drivers, strangers on the subway. And the ones who don't know about the biting will even try to touch it.

"No more crying, Zo Zo," Mom was saying as they got to the booth.

Zoe dialed back the wailing to a whimper.

"What happened?" I said.

"The you-know-what was out in front of that new restaurant on Eighty-Sixth," Jeanine said as she slid into the booth.

Zoe is terrified of this twenty-foot, blow-up rat with red eyes that shows up around the city whenever somebody hires nonunion workers. If you hire guys who aren't in the union, you can pay them less, but the union guys get really mad and park the rat outside your job so everyone knows you don't hire union guys. I'm not sure why it's a twenty-foot rat, except that it's gross and hard to miss.

"I wanna go home the other way," Zoe whimpered.

"Don't worry. We're going to the garage anyway," Dad said, groaning as he lowered Zoe into the booth. I don't know how my parents can lug Zoe around everywhere. She feels like she's made of bowling balls. It's not as if she's a big four-year-old either. Dad says it's because she's solid, which I don't get. Aren't we all made of the same stuff inside? How can her insides be more solid?

"What do we need the car for?" I said.

"Road trip," Mom said. "Apple picking. They have those Pink Ladies, the small ones we got at the farmers' market that time. And I found another farm on the way that makes its own ice cream."

"Cool," I said. "Do you know what flavors they have?"

"If you're asking if they have olive oil, I think it's unlikely," she said.

I had been. Ever since my parents took us to this Italian restaurant downtown that made it, I've been on a quest. I know olive oil ice cream sounds like it violates some basic law of the universe, but the weirdest thing is, when you taste it, everything you ever thought about ice cream gets completely turned around. *Vanilla* seems wrong. *Chocolate?* Crazy. Olive oil? What God put on the earth so we could turn it into ice cream. The whole experience really messed with me. I mean, if olive oil is really supposed to be made into ice cream, maybe we've been using other foods all wrong too. Like maybe there should be a steak-flavored yogurt.

"Sorry," Mom said, "but maybe they'll have some fabulous flavors they make with stuff from the farm, like pear or buttermilk."

"Not the same," I said.

"Get over it, nuddy," she said, swatting me with her scarf.

"Nuddy" is what Mom calls us when we're being thick. It's short for *nudnik,* which means "stupid" in Yiddish, a language her grandparents spoke and pretty much nobody else does anymore. I guess that's kind of the point. It's not like she wants people to understand what she's saying. Besides, "nuddy" sounds sort of nice the way she says it, and "moron" sounds bad no matter how you say it.

Mom tasted the soup and made a face. "Kreplach's cold."

"Zippo will reheat it," Dad said.

"It's busy. I don't want to bother him."

Jeanine pushed her untouched bagel across the table.

"What's wrong with you?" I said through a mouthful of egg.

"Ask her." She pointed at Zoe with one hand and showed me a Band-Aid on the other.

"She was taking too long," Zoe said, looking at me through the holes in her bagel halves.

"It doesn't matter how long she was taking," Dad said. "No biting ever. We use our words."

For some reason, when my parents talk to Zoe, it's always "we."

We use our words. *We* don't blow bubbles in our milk through a straw up our nose. *We* don't scream when we see a bald person.

"But I *did* use my words. I told her she was taking too long. The words didn't work."

I was with Zoe on this one. Sometimes Jeanine leaves you no choice. Besides, she's a drama queen. Most of the time, Zoe doesn't even break the skin.

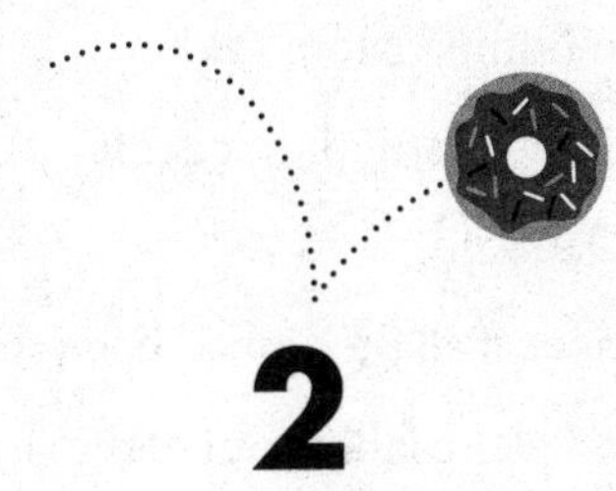

2

An hour later, we piled into the car and headed upstate on the highway along the Hudson River.

Somewhere in Westchester, my parents came clean. This road trip wasn't just about Pink Ladies and buttermilk ice cream.

"Surprise!" Dad said louder than you should ever say anything in a car, even if it is a station wagon.

"I don't understand," Jeanine said, leaning as far into the front seat as the seat belt would let her go. "You bought a house? Why?"

"Because we loved it," Dad said. The smile on his face was so big, it took up the whole rearview mirror.

Mom turned around, smiling the same huge smile. "And because it's beautiful."

"And because it's something different," my father added.

"So it'll be like that place on the Jersey Shore Sam's family has?" I said.

"That's a vacation home," Mom said.

"So what will this be?" I still didn't get it.

"A *home* home," Dad said.

That instant, it was as if all the air had been sucked out of the car. It felt like we were on a plane falling out of the sky, and those oxygen masks should have been dropping down from the ceiling of our car.

I couldn't speak. I looked at Mom, who was still turned around, and tried sending her messages with my brain to ask if this was really happening. And she must have understood, because she nodded.

"I don't feel good," Zoe said. I could feel her tugging on my sleeve, but I didn't do anything.

"Here, sweetie," Mom said as she reached back, pulled one of the old yogurt containers (also known as vomit buckets) off the armrest of Zoe's car seat, and handed it to her. Throwing up in cars, or really anything that moves, is normal for Zoe.

"You're gonna love it," Dad said, still grinning at us in the rearview mirror, the mirror I now wanted to chuck something at, shattering its stupid, happy face.

I think my parents kept talking. I'm not sure because all I could hear were my insides screaming as we dropped out of the sky.

"I don't understand. Why do we have to move?" Jeanine said,

her voice catching at the end so that "move" sounded like two words instead of one.

"We don't *have* to. We *want* to," Mom said.

How could I believe that when I'd never heard them talk about leaving the city? Not once. Not ever. Besides, would they tell us that we *had* to move even if that were the truth?

This had to be Oscar McFadden's fault.

Oscar McFadden was the reason my father had lost his job a month before. Oscar McFadden was the reason the bank where my father had worked since before I was born didn't even exist anymore. Don't ask me how. All I know is, the guy took the bank's money and put it into some crazy scheme that lost more than the bank ever had in the first place. He'd hidden what he was doing so Dad didn't have a clue, but once all the money was gone and the bank had gone up in smoke, it didn't matter what Dad knew. Just having worked in the same room as that crook meant no bank would ever hire him again.

"We really want something different," Dad said.

I hated the way he kept saying that. This wasn't something different. This wasn't even something. This was too big for something. It was everything.

What if Dad still had his job at the bank? Would he still want everything different then?

"Look, Dad and I have lived in New York our whole lives. We know what that's like. We thought it was time to try living someplace new," Mom said.

"Once you guys see the place, I'm telling you, you'll get it. And, Tris, just wait. The land is so beautiful. You're gonna love it," Dad said.

"You think *I'm* gonna love the dirt and the grass and the trees?" I said.

"Yes, Tris, *you*," he said, pointing at himself in the mirror.

What was he talking about? I wasn't a nature kid. I knew those kids. They were the ones always digging in the dirt looking for worms at the playground when we were little, and now they went to sleepaway camps where the toilet was just a hole in the ground.

"Wait till you see the pond!" Dad went on, all excited like he was talking about a wicked roller coaster and not a large hole filled with water. "You can swim in it in summer and skate on it in winter."

"I don't know how to skate," Zoe said, the words echoing out of her vomit bucket.

"We'll teach you," Mom said.

"I hate skating," I said.

"Why?" Dad said.

"You just go in circles. It's boring."

"Not on a pond. On a pond, you can go anywhere," he said.

"No, you can't. You're still skating in circles. They're just bigger circles."

"But we could fall through the ice," Jeanine said, suddenly panicked. "Zoe can't even swim. She'll drown."

"*I* swim," Zoe said.

"With water wings. Are you going to ice-skate in your water wings?" Jeanine said.

"Can I, Mommy?"

"Look, nobody needs water wings for skating because nobody's falling through the ice, got it?" said my mother, all serious now. She clearly wanted us to drop the whole subject.

"How do you know?" I said, glaring at her. I didn't care what she wanted. I might never care what either of my parents wanted ever again. And I didn't care about ice-skating on the stupid pond either, but I couldn't win an argument about moving.

"Have you thought about any of this at all?" Jeanine shouted as she burst into tears.

"Why's Jeanine crying?" Zoe said, peeking up from the vomit bucket. She still hadn't fully understood what was happening.

"Somebody will test the ice, okay? I promise. We'll make sure it's safe," my father said, as if Jeanine was actually crying because she was afraid of falling through ice.

"Like who? Professional ice testers?" I said, trying to force my face into a smirk and failing because smirking is impossible when you're dropping out of the sky.

"I don't know who," my father said, his smile finally failing. "All I know is that we're going to figure it out, and when we do, it's going to be great. The ice, the house, the land, all of it! And you're all going to love it!"

If it was all so great, and he knew we'd love it, would he have to keep telling us we would?

I knew great. Great was New York City. Great was Barney Greengrass. Great was Charlie Kramer, who'd been my best friend since we were in the Red Room in preschool together.

It was as if my parents had made up this story about some other family, one that loves ice-skating and nature and is bored of living in the greatest city in the world, and we were just supposed to play along and pretend that was us even though none of it was true.

Three hours later, Dad turned off Country Road 21B into woods so thick they cut out the sun.

"We're here!" he practically sang as we started up a steep, zigzagging dirt road.

But "here" wasn't where we were. "Here" was at the top of the mountain, and we were still at the bottom. We had another whole vomit bucket to go before "here."

Finally, we came out of the trees and rolled to a stop in front of a sagging, purple house.

Dad was wrong. We were here now. I was seeing it—the land, the house, and all of it—and I wasn't getting it. Not the broken-down, grape-colored house with windows popping out in all the wrong places. Not the shed that really was only half a shed because the other half looked like someone had burned it to the ground. Not the miles and miles of lonely sky and house-less, people-less fields and woods trapping us on top of this cliff.

"C'mon, guys, don't you want to come check it out?" Mom said.

Jeanine, Zoe, and I didn't move.

"Can I have your phone?" Jeanine asked, sniffling.

"Why?" Dad said.

"To call Kevin." Kevin Metz, chess champion, is the male version of Jeanine. They met in Gifted and Talented in kindergarten and have been best friends ever since.

"You can call Kevin on the way home. Now you're seeing the house," Mom said.

"Where are we?" I asked, looking out the window.

"Petersville," Dad said.

"Is there an actual town?" I didn't see another house anywhere.

"About six miles away," Mom said.

"How are we supposed to get there?" I said.

"Car or bike," Dad said.

"We need to get in the car just to get milk?" I said.

"What do you think of the house? Big, right?" Mom was smiling that huge smile again.

Clearly, that was a "yes" on needing the car to go get milk.

"No more sharing," Dad said as he and Mom got out of the car. "You guys each get your own room. Don't you want to go in and look around?"

Jeanine, Zoe, and I still didn't move. For once, I'm pretty sure we were all thinking the same thing: if we went inside, that was it. The house was ours. From the outside, it could still belong to someone else.

Mom opened the door to the back seat. "Come on! Come see."

"Why are the windows all different sizes?" I said, staying put.

"It's neat, right?" she said. "An artist and her husband built it. They wanted something completely original. Something that would surprise you."

"Were they color blind?" Jeanine asked.

Mom laughed. "No, the artist's name is Iris, you know, like the flower. Most of their furniture was purple too. Pretty zany."

"Is that code for crazy?" I said.

"They aren't crazy," Dad said. "We met them. They're great."

"Mmm, like everything else here," I said into my T-shirt.

Dad opened the back door on the other side. "Enough! Everybody out."

Jeanine, Zoe, and I obeyed but in slow motion, and we didn't go to the house. We just stood beside the car on the brown lawn. Even the grass looked unhappy to be there.

Jeanine leaned back against the car and studied the house. "Did they give it to you for free?"

"Of course not," Mom said.

"How do you know it's safe?" I plopped down on the grass next to Jeanine's feet. It wasn't just that I didn't want to get any closer to the house than I had to, I needed to stick with my side. This was us versus them, and we were going to lose—we'd already lost, even if Jeanine didn't realize it yet. And if we were going down—maybe even because we were—we had to stay together. Jeanine must have felt it too, because a minute later she slid down the car until she was kneeling next to me on the ground.

Dad blew his cheeks out like a chipmunk. He was definitely annoyed we didn't want to go in the house, but he didn't try to make us get up. Instead, he and Mom walked across the sad lawn and sat down on the porch stairs opposite us.

Zoe looked at my parents, back at us, and then climbed into my lap. She still didn't get the everything of what was happening, but even she knew there were sides and which was hers.

"What does an artist know about building a house anyway?" Jeanine said. "Was her husband an architect?"

"He worked for the postal service," my father said.

"What's it called when you're not supposed to go into a building because they're afraid it's going to fall on you?" I squinted up at a portion of roof that looked like it was working particularly hard to resist the force of gravity.

"Condemned?" Mom said.

"Oh, yeah." Jeanine nodded. "It's totally condemned."

"It's not condemned," Dad said. "It's completely safe. It just needs some work. It'll be fun."

"I don't understand," I said. "Neither of you knows anything about fixing up things." I guess the parents in the made-up family we were pretending to be were also really handy.

"We're smart. We'll figure it out," Dad said.

"You couldn't even put together Zoe's toddler bed," I reminded him. "And that came with an instruction manual and pictures. You didn't even need to know how to read."

"Fair point," he said. "But I think I learned a lot from that experience."

"And how are you going to have time to fix up the house and do a job?" I said.

"Easy. I'm not going to get another job."

"How's that going to work?" I asked. Mom hadn't cooked at a restaurant since I was born, and I was pretty sure we couldn't live on what she made catering a few parties every month.

"Yeah, don't you eventually need a job that pays you?" Jeanine said.

"We have savings. Plus, things are a lot less expensive out here, and your mom is going to start a business, so I'll help with that. Tell them, Kira."

"I'm going to open a restaurant!" Mom said, smiling her biggest smile, the one that goes all the way to the crooked tooth she doesn't like to let people see.

"China Palace?" Zoe said, jumping up.

"I don't think so, Zo Zo. I'm not going to serve Chinese food."

"But I love Chinese food."

"I know, but I'm going make food I like to cook. It will actually be the first restaurant in Petersville. Isn't that exciting?"

"There are no restaurants? How does it even qualify as a town?" I asked.

"Of course it's a town," she said. "But think how amazing it will be to open a restaurant in a place where there aren't any others."

That wasn't what I was thinking. What I was thinking was: What was wrong with the people who lived here that it had never occurred to anyone to open a restaurant?

We never did go inside that day. We just sat there on the ground till my parents gave up and told us to get back in the car. So I guess we won something.

Us: 1.

Them: everything else.

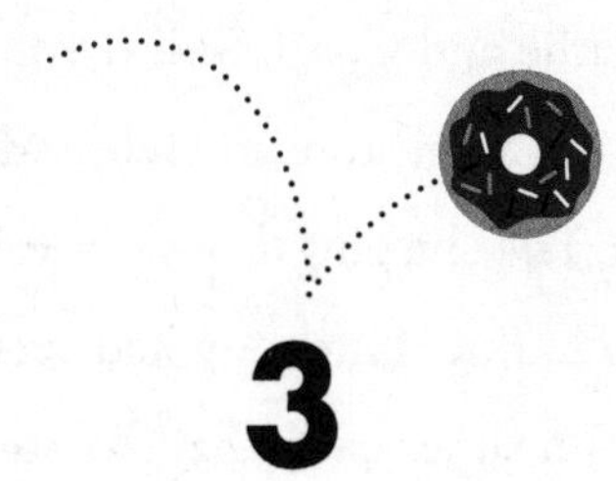

3

I didn't tell anyone we were moving, not even Charlie. He and I spent the whole day together that Sunday after we went to Petersville, and I didn't say a word about it. I couldn't. Just like going into the house would have made it ours, saying I was moving would have made it true. So I pretended I wasn't, and we played basketball till it got dark, practicing for the tryouts I'd never go to.

It helped that Charlie talks a lot, especially when he's worried, which he was. Charlie could go on forever about our chances of making the basketball team. The closer tryouts got, the more he talked about them. He was like Jeanine in spelling bee season, but unlike Jeanine, he was totally psyching himself out.

"Coach Stiles hates me," he kept saying that day as he shot and missed basket after basket.

“What are you talking about?” I said.

“I know Raul told him the crickets were my idea.”

Last spring, Charlie and Coach Stiles’s son Raul had bought a hundred crickets from a pet store and released them in the ceiling over our classroom. The chirping drove Ms. Patel so crazy, she sent us all home at lunch. But somebody had seen Raul and Charlie go into the classroom super early that day so they were called to Principal Danner’s office. Under questioning, Raul came clean, but Charlie denied everything.

“What did you expect?” I said.

“He got, like, two days’ detention. Boo-hoo. But my dad doesn’t work for the school. I totally would have been suspended.”

“No way. It so wasn’t a big deal. Everybody thought it was funny.”

“Whatever. Stiles still hates me. No way he takes me.”

“He will if the team needs you.”

“He wouldn’t take me if I were LeBron James. It’s just like my dad says: don’t tick people off because nobody’s gonna miss a chance to get you back.” Then he hurled the ball so hard it slammed into the backboard and boomeranged right back to him.

Charlie’s father is full of these cheerful fortune cookie sayings like, “Getting what you want isn’t about what you do but who you know,” and, “Life’s not fair. Get used to it.” I know them by heart because he says the same ones over and over.

Bottom line: Zane Kramer is a nuddy. But you can't tell your friend his dad's a nuddy. That's just something Charlie was going to have to figure out on his own. The problem was, Charlie wasn't figuring it out.

It wasn't his fault. You live with stuff long enough, it's bound to rub off. It happens to all of us. What had rubbed off on me was a serious chocolate addiction. At least eating chocolate makes you happy. What was rubbing off on Charlie was the idea that everything and everyone was out to get him. I hated seeing him going down that road, but I didn't know what I could do about it.

"Pass!" I called, running to the basket. Distraction wasn't a long-term solution, but it had been proven to work in the moment.

Charlie threw me the ball. I jumped and tossed. *Swish.*

Charlie chased the ball down, then stood on the free throw line dribbling, his tongue peeking out above his lip as he eyed the basket.

Charlie, age four, tongue peeking out, planted in a tiny chair outside the Red Room popped into my head.

"Hey, remember the water table?" I said.

Charlie stopped dribbling and looked at me. "The what?"

"The water table. In the Red Room?"

"Oh yeah." He grinned. "I loved the water table."

"Yeah, me too. So did Charlotte K, remember?"

He whistled. "Charlotte K. I can't believe you still remember her name."

I will never forget Charlotte K.

The day I pushed Charlotte K—she'd been hogging the waterwheel again—she fell, slicing her head open on the corner of the water table. In seconds, her sparkly T-shirt was soaked red. "Charlotte K is dying!" some girl screamed. And I believed her, because how could anyone lose all that blood and survive?

"I'm sorry! I'm so sorry!" I blubbered as Charlotte K was rushed from the room.

No surprise: Charlotte K wasn't actually dying, though nobody bothered to tell me. I didn't find out until I got home that three stitches in her scalp at the emergency room were all it had taken to snatch her from the jaws of death.

Charlie had been standing next to me at the water table, and even though he hadn't said anything, he hadn't left my side. He even crawled under the water table with me when I dove under there with paper towels to mop up the blood—it seemed the least I could do. Then, when it came time for yard, he refused to go because I couldn't. I had to stay inside and think about what I'd done (kill Charlotte K). Kylie and Maria explained to Charlie that this was my punishment, that he couldn't play with me, that I needed to sit alone to think about my evil, evil ways.

"Fine," he said and dragged his little chair just outside the classroom. "Then I'll stay here." And there he sat for all of yard, tongue glued to his upper lip, watching me, fifteen feet away on my own little chair as I bawled for poor Charlotte K (and myself).

Charlie Kramer was something different. Anything else would be something worse.

Charlie eventually found out we were moving from his mom, who'd found out from my mom. He couldn't believe I hadn't told him. I tried to explain about not saying it so it wouldn't be true, but he didn't get it. He was too mad. He seemed ever angrier that I hadn't *told* him I was moving than he was that I was *actually* moving, but I got why. Mad feels like it's going somewhere at least. Sad just sits on your chest making it hard to move or breathe. If I'd had the choice, I would have picked mad too.

At home, I went radio silent. I'm pretty sure my parents didn't even notice since Jeanine was in an all-out war and wouldn't stop talking, mostly about how she'd never become president if she went to a school with no G&T.

Whenever anyone asked Zoe about the move, she told them that we were leaving the city so Mom could open a Chinese restaurant. Her true feelings were clear from the number of times Mom had to pick her up early from preschool because she'd bitten someone.

Just so you know, I'm not saying my parents didn't notice my not talking to make you feel sorry for me. It's just a fact. When Jeanine's freaking out, it's hard to notice anything else. Besides, it was better that way since if my parents had noticed, they would have just kept pestering me to talk, which is about the worst thing you can do to somebody who needs to go quiet for a while.

I just kept thinking, if this move were really about wanting something different and had nothing to do with money, wouldn't my parents let us finish the school year? Or at least stick around until winter break?

Everybody thinks where they live is something special. Here's how I know the place I lived actually was: it sold in just three hours the day of the open house. In case you're lucky enough not to know, an open house is when complete strangers are invited in off the street to snoop around and see if they want to buy your home.

On November 3, my parents signed the contract selling our apartment. We wouldn't be kicked out until the closing though, and I figured we had at least a month because my parents hadn't even started packing. I hadn't counted on them cheating.

Did you know you can pay extra to get movers to pack your

stuff before they move it? Yeah, well, you can, and those guys are fast, because it's all just stuff to them. *Wrap. Box. Repeat. Wrap. Box. Repeat.* Smoothe Move was a packing machine. In just one day, everything that wasn't nailed down was in a box. Two-year-old Halloween candy? Check. Half a Slinky? Check. I watched one guy Bubble Wrap an ant trap without giving it a second thought.

I couldn't believe how fast everything was happening.

November 15, a month after we'd gone to Petersville for the first time, we'd be living there. We wouldn't even get one last Thanksgiving at home. No camping out on Seventy-Seventh Street with a thermos of hot chocolate to watch the balloons being blown up for the parade. Not this year. Maybe never again. At least Charlie's family had promised to come to Petersville to do Thanksgiving together like always.

Our last night at home, my parents took Charlie and me to dinner at Katz's on Houston Street. Number one hot dogs on the planet. And unlike Barney's, it's about as far from the Upper West Side as you can get and still be in Manhattan, so going there was a big deal.

In the car on the way downtown, Charlie and I made bets on how many hot dogs we'd put away. Six is my record. I did eat seven one time, but I don't count it because I had to use one of Zoe's buckets on the way home.

Charlie beat me that night by a good three dogs. I had to stop halfway through my second. It didn't taste right. Nothing tasted right. Not even the Dr. Brown's cream soda. I guess goodbyes, the everything-is-different-now, I-won't-be-around-next-time-you-almost-commit-murder-at-the-water-table kind of goodbyes, mess with your taste buds.

Next time I have a goodbye dinner, I'm going to pick some place I don't love the food.

We didn't get to Petersville till late that first night because Zoe had handcuffed herself to the refrigerator in our apartment. They were only toy cuffs, but she'd flushed the key down the toilet, and none of us could remember the secret to getting them open. Dad called the toy company's helpline, but even that took forever because the cuffs were really old, and the new ones had a different trick. Anyway, by the time he was transferred to somebody who knew how to open these handcuffs, he'd been on the phone for almost two hours.

Then, when we finally got to the house, it turned out that my mother had packed the house key in a box on the moving truck that wasn't coming till the morning. Zoe eventually got us in by squeezing through a cat door we found after stumbling around the porch in the dark looking for doors or windows that had been left unlocked.

Usually, I'm not into stuff about the universe speaking to you and all that, but sometimes when things happen in a certain way, it makes you think about why and what it means. You understand, right? If we'd all been dying to get into that house, wouldn't someone have remembered to take the key? Wouldn't one of us have remembered the trick to opening Zoe's handcuffs?

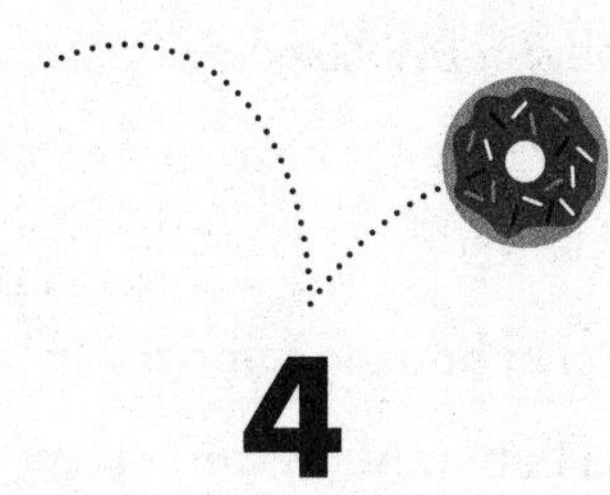

4

It doesn't bother me that my parents made me take the attic bedroom, even though it's pretty obvious from the rope ladder that before we got here the "attic bedroom" was actually just the "attic," the place people put things they wanted to forget but felt weird throwing away. What does bother me is that they think I'm stupid enough to believe that I got it because I'm the oldest and that it's some great privilege to sleep in a room where the ceiling slopes so badly it feels like an airplane. I may be a nuddy, but I'm not completely clueless. I'm the one sleeping in the attic because Zoe's too scared and Jeanine's too Jeanine.

On my way to the bathroom in the dark that first night, I missed the bottom two rungs of the ladder and landed hard on the hallway floor.

"Tris?"

It was Jeanine. I felt my way along the hall to her door. She was in bed reading *The Wolves of Willoughby Chase,* a flashlight balanced on her shoulder and Paws, her bear, tucked under her arm like he was reading too.

"Don't you have that book memorized by now?"

"It makes me feel better. And I can't sleep."

"Yeah, me too. The attic's got this really bad smell, and it's coming from this one spot on the wall right next to my bed."

"Your wall smells?"

"I don't think it's the wall itself. I think it's something dead trapped *inside* the wall."

"Uch. That's so disgusting. What made you even think that?"

"Probably the sound of all the not-dead mice running around in there."

"Ew!" She shivered.

"Hey, how long do you think it takes a dead mouse to stop stinking? I mean, eventually it has to run out of stink, right?"

"I guess it depends how long he's been there."

"Something tells me Mom and Dad aren't going to let me call Iris and ask her how long the attic has stunk of dead mouse."

"You can stay here if you want." Jeanine scooched over and shined the flashlight on the space she'd just made in the bed.

"Oh, okay. Thanks. One sec."

When I got back from the bathroom, I climbed into bed next to Jeanine. Then I just lay there listening to her breathe. She makes this tiny whistle when she inhales because she's got a little asthma, or severe reactive airway disease if you ask her. Anyway, I guess I'd kind of been missing it up in the attic all by myself. Don't get me wrong. I love not having to share a bedroom anymore, but I'd slept with that whistle my whole life or at least as long as I could remember, and now, even though it was gone, I couldn't get myself to stop listening for it.

I must have gotten bored just listening though because I found myself reading over her shoulder. "What's this about anyway?"

"What?"

"*The Wolves of Willoughby Chase*?"

She turned the flashlight around so it was shining right in my face. "You *really* want to know?"

I covered my eyes. "Yeah."

"Yeah? Yeah like 'whatever'?"

"No, yeah like yeah. I want to know what makes you read it over and over. Also, this part where the wolves attack the train actually seems good, you know, for a book."

"It is. *So* good," she said, shining the flashlight back on the book. "So you really want to know?"

"Are you kidding me? How many times are you going to make me say it?"

"Okay, okay." She turned off the flashlight. "So, it's about these girls. And they're left alone with this woman, who is *supposed* to take care of them while one girl's parents go on a trip. Anyway, the woman turns out to be evil and wants to steal the parents' money, and she locks the girls up in this horrible orphanage. Oh, and then there's a shipwreck and everyone *thinks* the parents are dead, but they're not and—"

"Wait, what about the other girl's parents? Where are they?"

"Oh, right, those parents *are* actually dead, and the aunt is super old and is getting really sick while the girls are locked up and starved and tortured in the orphanage."

"*This* is the book you love so much you've read it like a million times? It's like a horror movie."

"I guess it *is* kind of like one terrible thing after another, but then the girls fight back and eventually they save the old woman, and everything turns out okay. But it's the horrible stuff that really sucks you in."

Neither of us said anything for a pretty long time after that, and I actually thought maybe Jeanine had fallen asleep, but then she whispered, "Do you think we'll get to go back if it's really bad?"

"Home?"

"Yeah. You know, like if we show that we're trying, really trying, but we're still not happy here." Her voice was all shaky now, not at all like it had been when she was telling me about the book. "Do you think they'll let us move back?"

"I don't know." I guess unlike me, Jeanine hadn't been pretending to believe my parents wanted to move just because they wanted something different. She actually believed it.

"I know you don't *know* if they'd move back. But what do you *think*? If we're really not happy?"

What I *thought* was that even if my parents wanted to move back, they wouldn't have the money to. What I *thought* was that this, Petersville, was it for good. But what I *knew* was that Jeanine wasn't really asking me to tell her what I thought, even if she didn't realize it. Jeanine was asking me to tell her what she needed to hear to fall asleep on our first night in a place that was not and might never feel like home. So I did. "Maybe they'd let us move back. Definitely maybe."

"Do you think we should ask them?"

"Definitely not."

"Why? I'd feel better if I knew for sure we could go back if things weren't...working out here."

"If Mom and Dad know you're thinking we might move back, they're never going to believe you're really trying here."

"I guess you're right," she said and then took a big breath that caught a couple of times on the way in.

"Look on the bright side, we're not trapped in an orphanage starving while some evil woman tries to kill our parents and steal the family fortune, right?"

"Right," she said sadly and let her head fall onto my shoulder.

"You can read more if you want. I don't mind."

"Thanks. It helps." She turned the flashlight back on and leaned the open book against her bent legs. After a few minutes, I found myself reading over her shoulder again. She was right. All the horrible stuff did suck you in. One of the wolves had jumped through a train window and a passenger was fighting it off with a knife.

Jeanine must have known I was reading because when I got to the end of the page, she said, "We can start back at the beginning if you want."

"Okay," I said. I'd thought she'd meant we'd go on reading to ourselves, but when she flipped back to the first page, she began reading out loud, which was actually kind of nice because I could close my eyes and just listen and picture what was happening.

I must have fallen asleep because the next thing I remember is waking up to Jeanine drooling on my shoulder. She must have conked out while reading because the flashlight was still on and the book was crushed between us. Her room did smell better than mine, but she was hogging the one pillow so I turned off the flashlight and went back up to the attic.

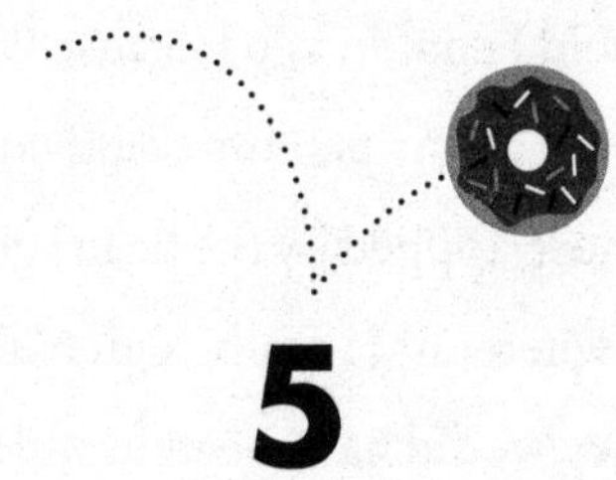

5

When I woke up that first morning, it was still dark and my bed was wet. I couldn't believe it. I hadn't wet the bed since I was two. It had to be just one more sign from the universe that I wasn't where I was supposed to be.

Then something dripped onto my nose and I realized that my wet bed was actually a sign that it was raining and that there was a hole in the ceiling.

Welcome to Petersville!

Since it was still early, I tried to sleep some more but it was too quiet, and I couldn't find a comfortable position out of the wet spot. So when the sky finally started to pink up, I decided to bike into town. Just because there wasn't a restaurant in Petersville didn't mean there was no bakery or bagel place.

Somehow, I made it down the rope ladder in the dark without breaking my neck or waking anybody. I wasn't interested in company or being told I couldn't go because it was too dark or too rainy or too whatever else my parents could come up with.

The rain had almost stopped by the time I got outside, but there were puddles everywhere, and I really regretted my decision not to wear socks since they would have been useful to soak up the mud seeping into my sneakers.

I ran across the lawn and around the back of the car.

Ugh. Dad had loaded my bike on the rack first. I was going to have to undo all the straps on each bike and drag everybody else's off to get to mine. If I'd known what it was going to take, I probably would have stayed in bed, but it was too late now. My shoes were already soaked. I might as well have something to show for it, something like breakfast.

Because I don't have a death wish, I walked my bike down Terror Mountain, my pet name for our driveway. Even walking though, I had a hard time keeping control of the bike, and by the time I got to the bottom, my shins were sore from banging them so many times with the pedals.

I walked the bike onto the main road, then climbed on and wobbled off. I hadn't ridden with cars before, and I kept turning around to check if one was behind me. My parents thought it was too dangerous to bike in city traffic, so I'd only ever ridden in Central Park on weekends when cars aren't allowed. Even though I didn't see any cars as I set out for town that morning, I was sure one was bound to whizz by any second, knocking me into some ditch too deep to climb out of.

But the cars never came, and the longer I rode without seeing any, the more I relaxed. It was actually easier than biking in Central Park. The road was smoother, and there were no people or strollers or other bikers. It was just me and the road and the woods all around. Flying downhill, I opened my mouth and whooped without knowing why, except that I wanted to, and nobody was around to tell me to stop.

I don't know how long I'd been riding when I started up a monster hill, but it must have been a while because when I finally came over the top, there was the sign for Petersville. That's when I noticed the train tracks headed like me toward the traffic light and a cluster of low buildings. They couldn't have carried a train in a long time because some sections were missing and others had been tarred over.

I got off my bike at the traffic light, even though there wasn't any actual traffic, car or people. Petersville was as dead as County Road 21B had been, so dead the place didn't even look real. It was more like one of those pretend towns they build for movies, and in this movie, something really bad had happened, and everybody had moved away.

The first three buildings in town were boarded up with plywood and had FOR SALE signs out front. Though Renny's Gas Mart, a convenience store with two filling stations, showed signs of life, I crossed the street to check out some place called Turnby's, hoping to find something better there than packaged coffee cake that had probably been sitting on a shelf since before Zoe was born.

Unfortunately, Turnby's wasn't a market or a bagel place or a bakery. I'm still not sure exactly what Turnby's is. Here's what was in the window that day: wool camping blankets, Silly Putty, fishing rods, socks, electric nose-hair clippers, a space heater, pipe cleaners, and candy necklaces. It was as if Mr. Turnby woke up one morning and said, "I'm going to open a store, and I'm going to sell whatever I feel like."

Next to Turnby's was the General Store, and the first and only thing I noticed about it was the large, handwritten sign in the window:

Yes, we do have chocolate
cream doughnuts!

Those have to be the best seven words you can read when you're starving and you've just moved to a town that it's pretty clear anyone who can has moved away from. Don't get me wrong. The strangeness of the sign wasn't lost on me. I mean, was that all they had? And if so, what about the store was general? But I was willing to focus on the positive: chocolate cream doughnuts!

All I had to do was wait till the store opened.

The General Store was the last building on that side of Main Street so I crossed back over to check out the largest building in town, a two-story brick house with a bright red door.

"Petersville Free Library," I read sadly on the sign over the door.

Books are okay, but you can't eat them.

Next to the library were two houses that must have been identical at one point but now looked like *Before* and *After* in one of those TV shows where people get strangers to come fix up their house. *Before* was covered in peeling, dirty paint and had broken windows and a mud pit front yard. Beside it, *After* exploded in blinding yellow with electric blue trim. A Gatorade-green lawn rolled out in front of the house, and a sign on the porch read: DR. CHARNEY, FAMILY CLINIC. *After* looked like it had been dropped on Main Street from another world, a happier, better world. Like me.

The last building in town—that's right, that was it!—was all by itself, far from the others, and if the General Store windows hadn't still been dark, I wouldn't have gone to see it.

Just past the clinic, the train tracks popped up again, and like last time, they and I were headed to the same place, the one-story cottage with wavy trim like Mom puts on gingerbread houses.

When we got there, the tracks set off for the back of the building, and I stopped out front. A Petersville sign hung over the front door, and long benches lined the wide porch. I leaned my bike against the porch steps and looked through one of the broken windows.

Inside were a barred ticket window, more benches, and a tree about my size growing out of a crack in the middle of the floor. Soda cans, candy wrappers, and paper bags filled the corners of the room.

It didn't surprise me that the train didn't stop in Petersville anymore. Why would it bother? Who wanted to come here? Besides, you wouldn't want to make it too easy for the few people left to leave.

When I turned around, a light had come on in the General Store, so even though it was raining again, I hopped back on my bike.

I was soaked by the time I reached the store, but who cared about a little water when there were chocolate cream doughnuts to be had.

"I'll take a dozen!" I called out, barely through the door.

"Eggs are in the cooler," said a small, wrinkled woman sitting at a counter at the back of the store. She had long, yellow-white hair and was studying a book of sudoku puzzles.

"Not eggs. Chocolate cream doughnuts." I pointed to the sign. Just saying the words made my stomach rumble so loudly the woman's head shot up, eyebrows raised.

After giving me a quick once-over, she went back to her puzzles. "No doughnuts."

"Are they not ready yet? I can wait."

"We don't make doughnuts anymore."

"Not ever?" The disappointment was crushing.

"Not ever."

"But the sign?" I pointed at it again with both hands.

The woman sighed, then closed her book. "Yeah, well, most people know better than to ask. Besides, I like 'em to remember," she said and grinned showing a mouthful of teeth that perfectly matched the color of her hair.

Now I knew why everyone had moved away. It was this woman. She was evil. First, she had taken away the town's doughnuts. Now she was shoving the memory of them down everybody's throat with that sign.

"I don't understand. Were they bad?"

"Were they bad?" She snorted and pointed to a frame on the counter.

I picked it up and wiped the glass. There was a newspaper clipping in it with the headline, "Small Town Store Hits It Big with Chocolate Cream Heaven."

This was just cruel. "So if they were so good, why don't you make them anymore?"

"Too much work. After that story, people came in here from all over, all hours of the day and night. Nearly drove me crazy. I really had no choice."

Just in case you think you don't get it, let me tell you, you do: the General Store's chocolate cream doughnuts were so good, and people liked them so much, they decided *not* to make them anymore.

"But weren't you making a lot of money from them if they were so popular?"

The woman waved me away like this question was so stupid she wouldn't even answer it.

"Do you sell anything like doughnuts?" I asked hopefully.

"I'm mostly just hardware now. And eggs." She pointed to the egg cartons stacked on the cooler behind me. "I got some chickens a couple of years ago and thought, 'Why not?' Won't find any better. Yolks are orange."

Was that good? I opened one of the cartons. The eggs looked like something out of Dr. Seuss, some green, some blue, some brown, all different sizes, including one no bigger than a marble. "Where are the white ones?"

"Different chickens."

"Oh," I said, pretending to understand. "Okay, I'll take these then."

They weren't doughnuts, but they had to be better than anything I'd find at the gas station.

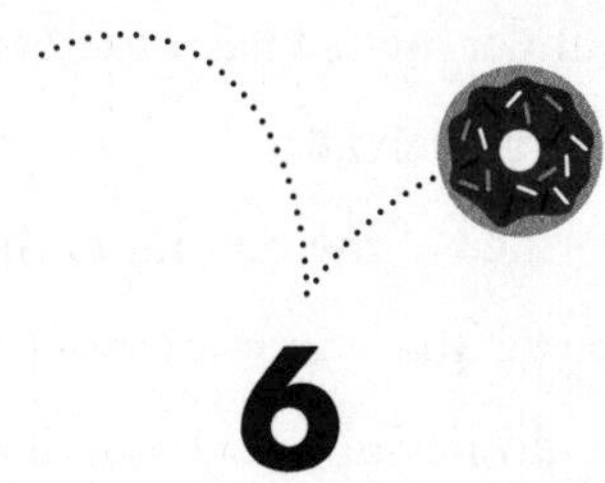

6

Rain was hammering the windows of the General Store, but I didn't think I should wait till it stopped. I'd been gone a pretty long time already, and there was a good chance my parents were up now, calling the local sheriff or ranger or whoever it is you call out here when kids go missing. So I put the eggs under my sweatshirt, tucked the sweatshirt into my jeans, and ran out into the rain.

Just as I reached the traffic light, lightning split the sky. *Crack!*

I jumped, then swerved. I managed to keep the bike under me, but I was still wobbling when I hit the hill on the edge of town. In seconds, I was flying...blind. The faster I went, the harder the rain came at me and the less I could see. I tried to slow down, but the brakes weren't holding because of all the water.

Suddenly, the bike stopped, and what I mean is, *only* the bike stopped. Me and the eggs, we kept going. We flew right over the handlebars and landed with a splat, the sound of some number of eggs being crushed under me as I fell into freezing cold water.

Somehow, since I'd ridden into town, a pond so big it deserved its own name had formed at the bottom of the hill. Lucky for me too, because landing in the water was way better than landing on the concrete would have been. I wasn't even hurt, just wet and cold.

When I stood up, I couldn't believe how high the water was, up past my knees. My bike was gone.

Just then, a horn honked, and a white truck pulled up next to me. The window rolled down.

"Need a ride," said the driver, a man with a tangled mop of brown hair and a beard that had taken over most of his face.

"Uh, no thanks," I said. "I'm okay. My parents are just behind me. They'll be here in a second." According to my mother, only kidnappers pull over their cars and offer kids rides.

The kidnapper laughed. "Uh, okay, kid, but I just came from behind, and there's nobody back there."

My face went hot, which was kind of amazing since I'd started to shiver.

"Look, it's no skin off my back if you want to drown in a flash flood. I was just trying to help," the man said, rolling up his window.

Did kidnappers give up this easily? It seemed unlikely. "Hey, wait, what did you say this is?"

"A flash flood. It's rained so much so fast, the ground can't absorb any more of it."

"I was on a bike. It's here somewhere." I waded back to where I thought I'd fallen.

"Ever heard of The Weather Channel?" He laughed as he got out of the truck. He went around to the back, pulled a long pipe off the bed, and began sweeping it back and forth through the water.

"There it is," he said a short time later, slapping the end of the pipe in the water.

I dove in and pulled up the bike. The seat was turned the wrong way, but otherwise it looked okay.

"You know you can't ride through this," he said.

"Yeah, I think I figured that out."

"Okay. Good luck then," the kidnapper said and got back in his truck.

"Hey, wait! Can I still get a ride?"

"I stopped to offer you one, didn't I?"

The first thing I did when I got into the truck was slide the carton of eggs out from under my sweatshirt. Amazingly, only three had broken, but I was covered in egg slime.

"Here." The kidnapper passed me a roll of paper towels. "Those from Winnie?"

"What?"

"The eggs. Did you get them at the General Store?"

I nodded.

He started the truck. "I love those eggs. Yolks are orange."

"Yeah, I can see that," I said, dabbing at the egg with a balled-up paper towel.

Even though the kidnapper drove really slowly, the truck kept sliding from one side of the road to the other. I gave up cleaning off and quickly put on my seat belt.

"Hydroplaning," the kidnapper explained. "Know what you're supposed to do when the car does that?"

I shook my head as the truck began to slide left.

"Gotta turn into the spin," he said, slowly turning the steering wheel to the left and then straightening us out just before we ran off the road.

I held tight to the seat belt with one hand and the door handle with the other.

"I'm Jim, by the way."

"Uh-huh."

"This is where you tell me your name."

"Oh, right. Jax," I said without missing a beat. I was taking the ride. He was going to see where I lived. No reason I had to give him my real name.

"Jacks, huh? As in more than one Jack?" He chuckled.

"No. Jax with an *X*."

"Okay, Jax with an *X*, you visiting?"

"Sort of."

"Haven't decided yet?" he said, winking at me.

"Something like that." I turned to look out my window, hoping it would discourage chitchat.

"So what do you think so far?"

No such luck. "Of what?"

"Town."

"I don't know. Not much to it—I mean…uh…" What kind of nuddy insults his kidnapper's hometown? "I just meant, it could use some more stores and stuff."

"I hear you," he said.

Maybe he was faking it, but he really didn't seem offended.

"The town is actually trying to get some more businesses in. In fact, people really want to see something go in the old station house."

"The place with the Petersville sign?" I said.

"That's right. The train used to run through town and stop there. We thought it should be put to some use, but nobody's sure for what."

"I once went to a restaurant in an old firehouse. It was really cool. They kept the pole and everything. You could do something like that?"

"You think we should put a restaurant there?"

"The town could use one. I mean, it seems like there's no place where people can get together, and that place would be perfect." I considered telling him about Mom's plans but decided it was best to keep Jim the Kidnapper on a need-to-know basis only. Just then, I saw our driveway fly by. "This is it!"

"What?"

"Here, here, here, stop here!"

"All right, relax. You sure you don't want me to take you up that hill. Looks like you still have a long way to go."

"No, it's fine. I'll just get out here, thanks."

Jim the Kidnapper pulled over. I got out and pulled my bike off the back.

"Okay, bye," I said, waving.

"Just wait one second." Jim climbed out of the truck holding a small tool. "Let me see that seat." After a minute of tinkering, the seat was back in its place.

"Thanks," I said.

"You're welcome, Jax. See you around."

"Yeah, right. See you around," I said, wondering where exactly you saw people around in Petersville. Did they hang out at Turnby's discussing the odd mix of products, trying to crack the code that tied them together? Judging from the chocolate cream doughnuts story, I couldn't imagine Winnie wanted a bunch of people chatting in her store even if they were buying stuff.

As I dragged my bike up Terror Mountain, I wondered how many state troopers my parents had out looking for me by now. After all, they'd woken up with me gone who-knows-where in the middle of a flash flood.

But there were no cars with sirens in front of the house when I finally made it there, just the moving truck. Wet cardboard boxes were already piled on the porch, and three guys in soaked SMOOTHE MOVE T-shirts were standing in front of them, studying the sky.

"Hey," one of them said to me as I came up the steps.

"Hi," I said.

"That your sister in there?" another asked.

"Yeah." I didn't have to ask who they meant.

"She's totally freaking out, man," the first said.

"Totally!" the second said.

"She yelled and then she cried and then she yelled some more," the third said.

"Yeah. She does that," I said.

"It's crazy," the first said.

"Totally," the second said again.

"And kind of scary," the third said with a shiver.

"Yup," I said.

Not only had my parents not been worried about me, they hadn't even noticed I was gone. And now that I was back, they barely seemed to notice that either.

"Does Tris know?" Jeanine shrieked when I came through the door.

"Know what?" I said.

"Go on. Tell him," she said.

"Right before we left the city, I got a call from the principal of Waydin Elementary. He seems so nice, really bright," Mom said.

"Get to the point!" Jeanine snapped.

"Jeannie," my father warned.

"Jeanine's upset because Mr. Kritcher doesn't want you two to start till second semester. He thinks it will make for a smoother transition," my mother explained.

"Do you even know how long that is? January! It's November. What are we going to do all that time?" Jeanine said.

I have to admit, I was with Jeanine on this one. What *would* we do all that time? I was all for an extra-long winter break, but given what I'd just seen of town, there was a good chance I'd die of boredom.

"I don't know," Mom said. "Start a project or something."

"Perfect! I love that idea," Dad said. "I'm making it official. Both of you will come up with a project, something all your own, that you can work on before school starts."

This was so much worse than dying of boredom.

"A project isn't school. How can we not go to school for two whole months?" Jeanine sobbed.

"Please, calm down," Mom begged, pressing her fingers to the sides of her forehead.

"And don't exaggerate. It's less than two months," Dad said.

"Isn't this illegal? Don't we have to be in school by law? What if I call the police and tell them my parents are keeping me out of school against my will?" Jeanine was pacing the kitchen now, and her voice was all crazy like we were playing her on the wrong speed. "What if I call Kevin's dad and ask him if there's some kind of court case he can file? What if I write to newspapers and news stations and—"

"*Sa-Sooo-Feeee!*" my father shouted so loud the third Smoothe Move guy, who'd finally gotten the courage to start bringing boxes in again, ran back outside.

Don't ask me what Dad yelled. All I can tell you is that it was French. Even though he grew up in New York, he spoke French at home because my grandmother is from France. Now his French never comes out unless he's really angry or talking to my grandmother—or both.

Jeanine doesn't speak French any more than I do, but right after Dad yelled, she ran out of the room too. Dad's French usually has that effect. Not just because he almost never yells, but also because getting yelled at in a language you don't understand is especially scary, which is strange when you think about it because, for all we know, he could be yelling, "I love croissants!"

"I need coffee," my mother said, searching through a box labeled *Pantry*. "Who's hungry?"

"Here, I got these." I put the eggs on the counter.

"Where are they from?" She opened the carton. "Wow! They're gorgeous. The ones that made it anyway."

"I went to town. The yolks are orange," I said as I headed upstairs to shower off egg slime and mud.

"Want me to make some?" she called after me.

"No!" I called back. How could they not have even noticed I was gone?

"I have other stuff I brought from home. You want something else?"

"Chocolate cream doughnuts," I muttered as I moped up the stairs.

"What?"

"Nothing! I'm not hungry."

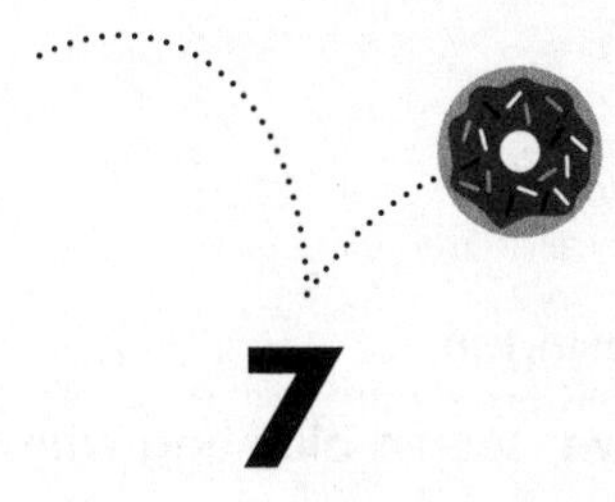

7

To: CKramerRocks@mar.com

From: JaxTLevin441@mar.com

Subject: Help!!!!!!!!!!!!!!!!!!!!!!!

Ow ow ooowww. Yes. Coyotes do really sound like that. I know this because I heard them circling our house last night. No lie. If you don't hear from me again, a mother coyote has fed me to her pups. I guess there could be worse ways to go. Uh, maybe not. Torn apart by coyote teeth has to be one of the top ten worst ways to die.

What's up?

T.

To: CKramerRocks@mar.com

From: JaxTLevin441@mar.com

Subject: Hello?

Did you get my email?

Coyotes closing in.

Have you ever seen a blue egg with an orange yolk? We've moved to Whoville.

Please send bagels FedEx.

To: JaxTLevin441@mar.com

From: CKramerRocks@mar.com

Subject: Re: Hello?

Are your parents ever getting you a cell phone? You and my grandparents are the last people on earth not using one. Try working the YOU DESTROYED MY LIFE BY MOVING ME TO THE MIDDLE OF NOWHERE thing. Maybe they'll feel bad enough to get you a phone.

Super busy getting ready for tryouts. My dad got me some private sessions with one of the coaches from Uptown Athletic Center so I could work on my shooting. Gotten way better already.

Send pics of the coyotes.

What's up with the eggs there? We'll bring bagels when we come for Thanksgiving. Where do you go for fun up there in Peter's Village?

For the next two days, I did nothing except unpack boxes and think about chocolate cream doughnuts.

Did the doughnut witch use milk chocolate or semisweet or dark? Was the cream airy like mousse or thick like pudding? Did she glaze the doughnuts or sprinkle them with powdered sugar?

The second night, when I couldn't take it anymore, I went downstairs and searched all sixty-seven of my mother's cookbooks while I finished off the apple crisp we'd had for dessert.

Not even Roland had a recipe for chocolate cream doughnuts. I guess it's hard to make fried dough presidential. I'm sure I could have found one on the internet, but you never know about recipes you find online. Besides, I wasn't interested in making just any chocolate cream doughnuts.

On the third day, my parents announced we were going to the library. Jeanine needed books for her project. Of course, she had it all figured out already and was raring to go. She was so fired up, she'd even forgotten about her plan to put my parents under citizen's arrest for keeping us out of school.

"It's a field study of the land around our house," she explained on the drive to the library. "First, I'll do a map. Then I'll mark the topography, you know, where the land rises and falls and then—this is the coolest part—I'll identify and label all the trees, plants, and animals with their common and scientific names!"

"Cool!" I was hoping my enthusiasm for Jeanine's project would keep anyone from asking about mine.

"Sounds fantastic," Dad said. "Zoe? What are you looking for?"

"Fairy dust."

"I was thinking books."

"You didn't say that. You said, *looking for*, and I'm *looking for* fairy dust because the happy thoughts aren't working." Zoe had been watching this old Peter Pan movie nonstop. Now all she could talk about was filling her mind with happy thoughts so she could fly, which, I guess if you ask Peter Pan, is all it takes.

"I don't think they have fairy dust at the library," Mom said.

"Can we make some?"

"We'll see."

"When we get home?"

"We'll see."

"Tawatty Tawatty Dabu Dabu hate 'we'll see.'" Zoe smacked the back of Mom's seat with her vomit bucket.

Tawatty Tawatty and Dabu Dabu are Zoe's imaginary friends. We have no idea what they look like, but they must be very small because she's always pulling them out of her pockets. It's also possible they're attached in some way because one never appears without the other, and she usually refers to them as the unit, Tawatty Tawatty Dabu Dabu.

Mom turned around and snatched the bucket out of Zoe's hand. "You know what *I* hate? When Tawatty Tawatty Dabu Dabu make a mess. No fairy potion project unless I specifically say so, got it?"

"Fairy dust, not fair potion."

"Did you hear what I said?"

"*I* did," Zoe said.

"And Tawatty Tawatty Dabu Dabu?" Mom said.

Zoe shrugged.

"Behave yourself," Mom said and handed Zoe back her bucket.

"What about you, Tris?" Dad called over his shoulder. "You come up with a project yet?"

There it was. The question I'd been dreading.

"Yeah," I said, drawing out the word to buy time.

The truth was, I had nothing. I blamed the doughnuts. I'd tried. I really had. I'd sat for hours staring at a blank sheet of paper, but nothing came. Nothing, but those stupid doughnuts. Even now, with my brain spinning to give me something, anything, that's still all there was.

"So? What is it?" Mom said.

"Chocolate cream doughnuts," I said before I could stop myself.

"The ones you were telling us about?" she asked.

"Uh-huh?" I said hopefully. It had been an explanation, not an answer, but if they were willing to accept it as one, that worked for me.

"How can a doughnut be a project?" Jeanine said.

Excellent question. How *can* a doughnut be a project?

"Sounds like a project to me," Mom said. "Tell me more."

"I can't. I'm still figuring it out."

"Can't wait till you do," Mom said.

"Yeah, me neither," I said into my jacket.

At least now I had a good excuse for spending every waking second thinking about chocolate cream doughnuts.

When we got to town, I told my parents that I had some "research" to do at the General Store and that I'd meet them at the library.

The store looked the same as it had the first time I'd been there: dark and empty except for Winnie. She was in the back stacking egg cartons.

"Hi," I said.

I waited for her to say something back, but when it was clear she wasn't going to, I went on. "Those eggs were really good." I paused again, but Winnie just kept stacking cartons like I wasn't even there. "My whole family thought so."

Still nothing.

"And you were right. Those yolks *were* orange. I mean, like *really* orange. I've never seen that before."

That's when she finally stopped and turned around. "It's because my chickens spend their days outside in the sunshine eating plants like God intended."

I wasn't sure what she meant. Did God bless you with better eggs if you were kinder to your chickens? I must have looked as confused as I was because then she said, "See, the sunlight and the chlorophyll from the plants give the yolk that orange color. Those nasty, pale, tasteless yolks mean the chickens don't go outside."

"Wow, that's really interesting," I said.

Winnie rolled her eyes. "You going to buy some more or what?"

"I actually wanted to ask you some questions about those doughnuts you used to make," I said, pointing to the sign.

"Oh, goodie."

"I just wanted to know if maybe, uh, if maybe I could have the recipe," I said quickly.

"*My* doughnut recipe?" She poured herself a mug of coffee from a thermos on the counter.

I nodded.

"Why?"

It was a simple question, but I panicked.

As she watched me stammer, she smacked a packet of sugar against her hand like Danny Delaney from Little League used to do with his bat right before he tried to hit you with it.

After a couple of false starts, something began to spill out. "See, I know they're your doughnuts, but since they were so popular, they're also part of the town too, you know, like its history, and I just moved here and I thought that making the doughnuts would be a way of sort of getting to know the town."

I'd barely finished talking when Winnie burst out laughing, spewing coffee all over me. You'd think if you laughed in somebody's face and spat a hot beverage at him, you'd apologize, but no. Winnie just went right on laughing till she was gasping for breath like she was having a heart attack. And I just had to stand there and take it while she laughed in my face with the coffee all over it.

"Oh, I needed that," she said when she finally came up for air. She dabbed at the corners of her eyes with a napkin, then handed one to me. "Now, why do you really want the recipe?"

"Fine. Fine!" I snapped. I was over trying to get on her good side. What was the point? She clearly didn't have one. She was the evil doughnut witch of Petersville. "I just want one! Okay? My parents forced us to move here, and as far as I can tell, the best thing about this place is those doughnuts, so I just want one, okay?"

"Okay, okay. You just want one." She looked like she might burst out laughing again any second.

"That's not all," I said.

"There's more? You going to tell me now you think you can cure cancer with my doughnuts?"

"No. I was going to tell you that my parents are forcing me to come up with a project I can work on till I start school here, and I've decided your doughnuts are it."

"A doughnut's not really a project."

"I know! I know! A doughnut isn't a project. I get it."

"So I'm still not clear on how my recipe would help?"

Neither was I exactly, but an idea had begun to form right there as I'd been talking. "What if my project was bringing the chocolate cream doughnut back to Petersville?"

"What do you mean?"

"You said you don't want people to forget the doughnuts, right? But eventually they will, unless they can still have them."

"I guess, but I told you I'm not making—"

"I know. But *I* could make them. I could make them and sell them. Like a hot dog guy. Only I'd sell doughnuts."

"Let me get this straight: *You* want to make and sell *my* doughnuts?"

"Uh-huh."

"And how are people gonna know they're *my* doughnuts?" she asked like she'd just caught me cheating at cards.

"We can say it right there on the sign."

"Say what exactly?"

"Whatever you want. Winnie's Chocolate Cream Doughnuts. The General Store's Famous Doughnuts. Winnie's Heavenly Doughnuts."

"The General Store's Famous Doughnuts sounds pretty good," she said, nodding.

"So it's a deal?" I held out my hand for her to shake.

Winnie crossed her arms. "Not so fast. I can't just give you the recipe."

"Why not?" I should have known it couldn't be that easy.

"'Cause I don't know if you can bake. You need to make me something."

"You mean like a tryout?"

"That's right. Like a tryout, so I know you're good enough."

"Uh, okay. What do you want me to make?"

"Some kind of sweet. If I like it, I'll give you my recipe."

"Deal," I said, and this time, she shook my hand.

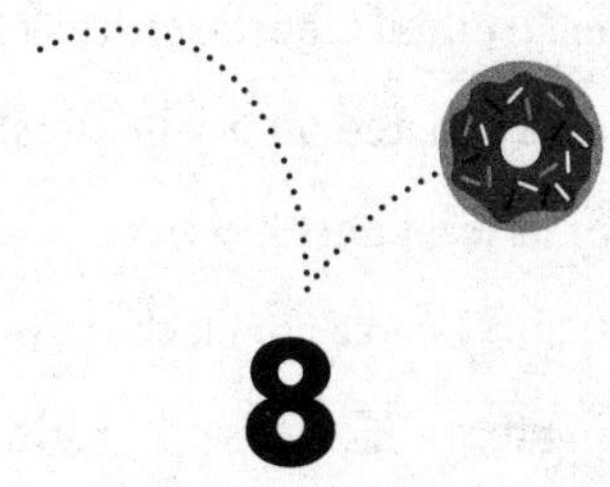

8

I found everybody sitting around a table in the library's reading room. Jeanine was deep into a book called *Rodents of North America*, while Zoe, Mom, and Dad were flipping through cookbooks and old cooking magazines.

"Mmm. Let's put this on the menu," Zoe said, holding up a photo of a glass filled with pink cream.

"Oh, I love fool," Mom said. "But it's only good when raspberries are in season, so I wouldn't put it on the regular menu."

Mom had decided to spend the winter experimenting with recipes for her restaurant, and then she'd look for a space in the spring.

"Couldn't you just make it with other fruit?" I asked.

"Not really. It only works because the raspberries fall apart when you mix them into the whipped cream."

"Are we leaving soon?" I wanted to get home to plan what to make Winnie. I'd already nixed chocolate chip cookies. Not enough wow. Maybe I'd email Charlie and ask him what he thought I should make since he'd tasted all my greatest hits.

"I want to stay for at least another hour," Mom said. "These old magazines are great, and I can't check them out."

"Go find something to read," Dad said. "Kids' Room is in the back."

On my way to the Kids' Room, I stopped at a computer to check my email. Since we'd moved, I couldn't stop checking it.

Big surprise: nothing from Charlie this time either. He was acting as if I was asking him to send smoke signals. It's not as if he couldn't check his email right there on his cell phone. So I *couldn't* text. What was the big deal?

I'd been trying to keep myself from sending him another email until he emailed me back, but I really wanted to know what he thought I should make Winnie.

To: CKramerRocks@mar.com
From: JaxTLevin441@mar.com
Subject: Hey

Guess what? Since we're not starting school, my parents are making me and Jeanine do these projects so I'm starting a doughnut business. Long story. I'll tell you everything at Thanksgiving. Maybe you can help??? For now, I just need to know which of my desserts you like the best, not including the peanut butter–white chocolate chip cookies.

The peanut butter cookies were definitely Charlie's favorite but plenty of people don't like peanut butter or white chocolate, so they were way too risky. You'd be surprised. There are some serious white chocolate haters out there. I don't get it.

When I got to the Kids' Room, I headed straight for a pile of lumpy beanbags by the windows. I've never been a napper, but I hadn't been sleeping. It wasn't just the doughnuts. The house, also known as the Purple Demon, talked a lot more than our apartment ever did. Clanging, creaking, moaning—different nights, different sounds. But her message was always the same, and I heard it loud and clear: *Get out!*

Halfway to the beanbags, I stopped in front of a table with a bunch of books on display to look at one with a basketball on the cover.

"It's good," someone said.

I looked around the room.

Tucked behind the door was a boy, lying on a bunch of beanbags, several books open on the floor in front of him. Everything about him was long from his arms and legs to his chin and his shaggy, black hair.

"Oh, thanks. Uh, what's it about? I mean, you know, other than basketball." I was hoping he didn't think I sounded as dumb as I thought I did. I couldn't have cared less about the book, but I was pretty excited to be speaking to a real-live kid in town.

"This high school basketball team that's really awful and how they end up winning the state championship. It's the fourth in the series. They're all really good though." The kid spoke like someone was timing him. "Each book follows a team in a different sport, and each time the team has to get through something hard, like an injury or a scandal or something, so they can come together and win, but then sometimes they don't win, and then that's sort of the point too, you know?"

He stopped and waited for me to give some sign that yes, I did know, and as soon as I did, he started right back up where he'd left off.

"I think the first one was about a swim team or maybe that was the second." He kept speed talking, but as he did, he stood up, crossed the room, and pulled a book from a shelf like he'd had its location memorized. "Yeah, this is the one. *Both Hands.* You should start with this." He handed it to me.

"Great. Thanks."

"So, you into basketball?"

"Yeah." I was relieved we were moving on from books to sports.

"Yeah, me too, but mostly just to watch. I really only play ice hockey."

"On a team?" Nobody I knew played ice hockey. Up until that point, I honestly thought the only kids who played lived in Canada, Minnesota, or one of those other states where it's cold like ten months a year.

"Uh-huh. It's pretty big here."

I could tell by the way he said "here" that he knew I was from somewhere else.

"I don't play," I said. "I was hoping that maybe there was a basketball team I could try out for."

"Sorry."

"No team?"

"No, there's a team, but all the good kids play hockey so the basketball team's...um, kind of..."

"Sad?"

"Pretty much."

Great, I was going to play on a sad basketball team with all the unathletic kids. Perfect.

"Can't you skate?" he asked like he'd never met somebody who couldn't.

"A little, but I don't even know the rules of hockey."

"You play soccer?"

I nodded.

"Not that different. I could show you. There's an open sticks and pucks session every weekend at the rink in Crellin. No rink here, but plenty of places to skate when it gets cold enough. Hey, you hungry?" he asked like it was part of the hockey conversation.

It took me a second to catch up. "Uh…" I wasn't hungry at all. Mom had made apple pancakes that morning. "Sure."

The boy led me back through the library to a small office behind the circulation desk.

"My mom works here," he said as he poked around the shelves of a mini-fridge in the corner of the room. "I'm Josh."

"Tris."

"Like for Tristan?"

"Yeah. My parents found it in some name book I wish they'd never bought."

"I don't know. Tristan was a knight at King Arthur's Round Table, which is pretty cool, and he was a better fighter than just about all the other knights except Lancelot."

"Who?"

Josh's face went tight, and he ducked his head behind the fridge door. "Sorry. He was just another big-time knight for King Arthur."

Josh went quiet for the first time since we'd met, and it was clearly not a good sign. What had I done and how could I fix it—quick?

"I guess you end up reading a lot if your mom's a librarian, huh?" I said. "We end up eating a lot 'cause my mom's a chef."

It must have worked because when Josh pulled a block of cheese from the fridge, he was smiling again.

"Get this. I know a guy named Michael Michael," he said.

It took me a second to retrace our conversation back to names. Ideas seemed to ping around Josh's mind like balls in a pinball machine.

"So, wait, Michael is his first and last name?"

"Yup. Mr. Michael Michael." Josh pulled a cutting board and box of crackers off the top of the fridge.

"I can top that. I know a girl named Sailor."

"Like on a ship?" he asked as he sliced cheese.

"She was in my sister's class."

"That's not right. Sailor's not even a real name." He handed me a cracker with cheese.

"I know. It's like child abuse."

"Yeah, like what if parents wanted to name their kid something like…Snot? That should be flat out against the law."

"Why would anyone want to name their kid Snot?" I said, laughing so hard bits of cheese flew out of my mouth.

"I don't know." Josh was laughing now too. "Why would someone want to name their kid Sailor?"

Josh and I spent the next hour eating cheese and crackers and coming up with a list of names we thought should be outlawed. A few times, we laughed so hard his Mom had to come in to tell us to keep it down.

When it was time to go, Josh filled out a library card for me and checked out *Both Hands* on it. He was sure I was going to love it. I wasn't, but I thought I should at least give it a shot.

"Hey," I said as I was leaving. "You know the General Store?"

"Sure," he said.

"You ever taste those doughnuts she used to make?"

"Oh, yeah."

"Were they really that good?"

"Not good," he said. "Life changing."

Life-changing doughnuts?

I had no idea what that meant, but I had to find out.

When we got home that afternoon, I finally had an email from Charlie:

To: JaxTLevin441@mar.com

From: CKramerRocks@mar.com

Subject: Re: Hey

What are you talking about? Kids can't start businesses. It's like against the law or something because businesses need insurance and have to pay taxes. How many twelve-year-olds do you know paying taxes?

I slapped the laptop closed.

The first email Charlie sends me in days, and he's telling me I can't start a business? And what did Charlie know about taxes? This had Zane Kramer written all over it. Why did Charlie have to tell his dad what I was doing anyway?

In my head, I wrote back: *What about lemonade stands? Why can't kids pay taxes?*

I opened the computer and hit Reply. But then I just stared at the screen. What was the point? Charlie would just keep repeating whatever his dad told him. I wouldn't even really be emailing with Charlie then.

I hit Delete and shut the computer.

He hadn't even told me what dessert I should make for Winnie.

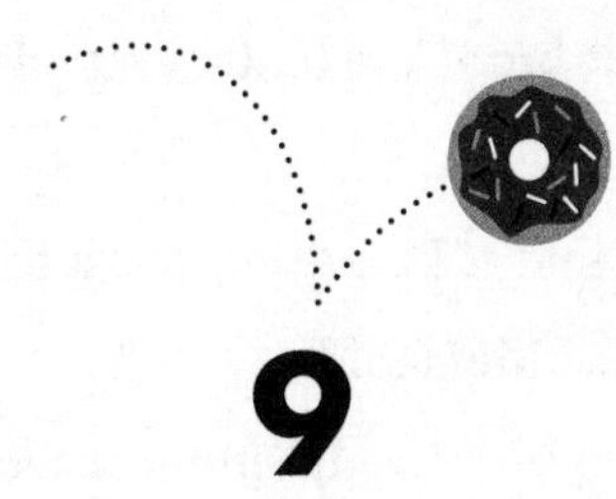

9

The day after we went to the library, it was so cold I could see my breath. I'm not talking about outside. I'm talking in my room, still in bed.

I ran to the window to close it, but it wouldn't budge, obviously part of a new plan by the Purple Demon to freeze us out.

I shoved my pillow in the window, layered up, and let myself down to the ladder through the hole in the floor.

Mmm. Mom was baking bread.

We never had homemade bread before we got to Petersville, but then Mom figured out it took her almost as long to drive to the nearest bakery as it did to make her own. At first, she just made simple stuff, like sourdough and whole wheat, but soon we were having sweet potato rolls, pumpkin biscuits, and hazelnut scones with homemade peach and strawberry butters. None of us were surprised when she announced she'd decided to serve a different homemade bread and butter every day when she opened the restaurant.

"Corn bread?" I said as I came into the kitchen.

"Close. Semolina," Mom said.

She and Jeanine were already sitting at the table eating breakfast. Even though there were no windows open in there, it was almost as cold as it had been in the attic.

The Purple Demon is a mad genius.

"Is the heat working?" I said.

"I think so." Mom handed me a plate of scrambled eggs and a thick slice of steaming bread with apple butter. "Houses are always cooler than apartments. It's much healthier. When it's too warm, it's the perfect environment for bacteria to flourish. That's why people are always sick in the city."

"Who was always sick?" I said.

"Don't you remember when we all got strep last winter?"

"Yeah, so? Don't people get strep in Petersville?"

"I'm sure they do, but it doesn't travel as fast because...because the bacteria can't move as well through the cold."

"Did you just make that up? Because it really sounds like you just made it up as you were saying it."

"Look, I may not completely understand the science behind it, but I know it's better not to keep your house too warm."

"*Too* warm, maybe. But how about *at all* warm? I mean, look at Jeanine."

Jeanine was sitting at the kitchen table with a sleeping bag around her bottom half, a bathrobe around her top half, and a ski mask.

"I don't mind," she said. "It keeps me awake. I've read seven hundred sixty-five pages since yesterday."

"That's great, honey," Mom said.

Sometimes my mother's completely clueless. The only reason Jeanine was able to read that much was because, unlike me, she still couldn't sleep. Whenever I passed her room in the middle of the night on the way to the bathroom, she was up, reading by flashlight.

"Where's Dad?" I asked.

"Upstairs. He's really excited about this new idea he has for a pulley system to schlep stuff up the stairs."

"Oh. That's kind of cool, I guess."

"I think so—and definitely better than the intercom idea. I really do think you need to be a licensed electrician to do that kind of wiring."

Now that the unpacking was done, Dad had a lot of free time, and he'd been spending it on these home improvement ideas he kept coming up with. Some actually weren't half-bad, but all required skills he hadn't picked up at the investment bank. Eventually, he'd be helping with the business side of the restaurant, but since there was no business side yet, the only way to help was by eating, which could only take up so much time.

"Zoe and I are headed to Crellin. Any takers?" Mom said.

Jeanine shook her head without looking up from her book.

"No thanks," I said. "Can I bake something?"

"What were you thinking?"

"Molten chocolate cake. I have to show the woman at the General Store I'm worthy of her doughnut recipe."

Mom laughed. "Sure, go ahead. Just remember to turn off the oven when you're done. And make a double batch so there's some for tonight."

I'd settled on molten chocolate cake for three reasons. First, I didn't know much about Winnie's tastes, but I thought I could be pretty sure she liked chocolate. She was weird, but I didn't think she'd have gone to the trouble of creating a recipe for chocolate cream doughnuts when she didn't like chocolate. Second, I'd never met anyone who didn't flip for my mother's molten chocolate cake. Third, other than chocolate chip cookies, I'd had more practice making it than anything else.

As soon as Mom and Zoe left, I turned on the oven and took

out the ingredients; a saucepan for melting the chocolate; and ramekins, the little cups we use for making mini cakes. You have to make mini molten cakes because the cake is so gooey, a big one will fall apart. I learned that the hard way.

I was especially careful not to burn the chocolate because, in case you don't know, burned chocolate tastes like metal and looks like dog food, and we didn't have enough to make another batch. I was also super careful measuring out the sugar and flour. Really, a clump more or less won't ruin anything, but I needed these to be perfect.

Twelve minutes in the oven is usually just enough to get the crackly shell on top that lets you know the cakes are done. That day, because I kept checking and letting cold air in, it took almost twenty.

As soon as the cakes were cool enough, I popped them out of the cups and tasted one. The hot, gooey center, more batter than cake, oozed out onto my tongue.

Shazzam! Taste bud happy dance all around my mouth. Perfect. So perfect that when I finished eating one, I had to go into the living room to keep myself from eating another.

"Can I have one?" Jeanine called from the kitchen. She hadn't said a word the whole time I'd been cooking.

"No!" I called back.

I hadn't forgotten about her telling my parents that doughnuts couldn't be a project after I'd said her project sounded cool, which it didn't. The day my parents told us we were moving to Petersville, it was us versus them for the first time ever. And I'd thought it would stay that way, at least for a little while, but Jeanine had already gone back to her own side, the one that only has room for her.

"I can't have just one?" she shouted.

"They're for my project!"

"I thought your project was doughnuts!"

"It is, but I need to give a molten chocolate cake to Winnie to get the doughnut recipe."

"Was that English?"

"I just have to give one to somebody! Okay?" I yelled.

"Come on!"

"They're for dessert tonight too!"

"That still leaves five!"

"Fine! Have one!" I flopped onto the couch. She wouldn't have let up until I gave in, so what was the point of going another twenty rounds, especially when I didn't actually have a reason, or at least not one I'd tell her?

I pulled some blankets over me and started reading *Both Hands*, the book Josh had made me take out of the library.

I don't know how long I was sitting there, but before I knew it, I'd read almost forty pages. Normally, I don't get through more than a couple without thinking about what we're having for dinner or checking where the chapter ends, but I'd been too focused on whether Jack—he was the kid in the book—was going to make the state swimming finals to think about anything else. Jack had just won regionals when Dad came through the living room carrying his brand-new toolbox.

"What are you doing?" I asked.

"Fixing that leak in your room. I checked it out the other day. Guy at the hardware store says it shouldn't be too complicated. Just give me a hand getting the ladder out of the shed?"

"Sure," I said.

When I came back, Jeanine was lying in my spot on the couch.

"It's warmer here," she said.

"It's warmer there because I was sitting there." I ripped one of the blankets I'd been using out from under her. Then I got my book and sat down to read in one of the armchairs.

Before long, we heard banging above us.

"What's that?" Jeanine said.

"Dad."

"On the roof?"

"He's fixing the leak in my room."

"Do you know how long that's going to take? I'm trying to get some work done here."

"I'm pretty sure he feels the same way."

She stuck her tongue out at me through the mouth hole in the ski mask, then went back to her book. I could tell she wasn't getting much reading done though, because after every bang, she looked up and gave the ceiling a dirty look.

If you want to know the truth, I couldn't tune out the noise either, but I knew it would drive Jeanine bonkers to think I could when she couldn't, so I went right on pretending.

After a while, she slammed *Conifers of the Northeast* shut, unzipped the bottom of the sleeping bag, stuck out her feet, and stood up. "That's it!" Then, still wearing the sleeping bag, bathrobe, and ski mask, she slid her feet into her boots and hopped out the back door.

Almost immediately, the noises stopped. Then came a loud thud that shook the house and a scream.

I jumped up and ran out the door.

Outside, Dad was lying on the ground, his face white.

"What happened?" I said.

"It's not my fault!" Jeanine said, kneeling beside him.

I dropped to the ground on the other side. "Are you okay?"

Dad sat up slowly.

"He's fine," Jeanine said. "Right, Dad? You're fine."

"I think so?" he said, not really sounding convinced. "Just my head."

Jeanine pulled off her ski mask and grabbed my father's hand. "Your pulse is pretty fast."

"I'm okay."

"Can you get up?" I said.

"He shouldn't move," Jeanine said. "What if he has a spinal injury?"

"You just said he's fine. Now he has a spinal injury?"

"You know, guys, I really think I'm okay to go inside."

"See!" I said.

"Fine. But don't blame me if he's paralyzed," Jeanine said.

We helped my father to his feet and slowly led him into the house. Jeanine made him lie on the couch, got some ice, and told him to put it on his head.

"You sure you're okay, Dad?" I asked.

"Huh?" he said like I'd just woken him up.

"You okay?" I said again. Something about his eyes didn't look right.

"Yeah," he said, but he still didn't sound sure. "Just my head."

"Do you know what you hit it on?" I was worried that maybe he'd hit a rock, but there wasn't any blood.

"Hit it?"

"Yeah, when you fell," I reminded him. Now, I was beginning to worry.

"Oh." He squinted like he was trying to see something far away.

"Yeah, you were on the roof trying to fix the leak, remember?" Jeanine said.

"Oh, yeah," he said even though it was obvious by now that he didn't.

"Um, Dad, why don't you just keep that ice on your head. We'll be right back," I said. Then I grabbed Jeanine's wrist and pulled her into the kitchen with me. "He must have a concussion. Should we call an ambulance?"

Jeanine nodded. For once, she didn't seem to know what to say.

I turned to the wall behind me where a phone should have hung and would have hung if we were still at home, but this wall was blank. The landline still hadn't been put in.

Jeanine ran out of the room. She was back a minute later with my father's cell phone and handed it to me.

For a second, I just stared at her, blown away she didn't want to make the call herself. Then I dialed 911 and waited for it to ring.

Nothing. No sound at all.

I looked at the screen. Not even one bar.

I showed Jeanine the phone. "No reception."

"Is anybody there?" my father called.

I poked my head through the doorway to the living room. "Yeah, Dad, we're here."

He sat up. "I think I hit my head."

"Oh, yeah? Do you remember what happened?"

Silence.

"Okay, then why don't you just keep that ice on it."

"Oh, okay," he said and lay back down.

It was like talking to a little kid, a not-so-smart little kid, and that kid was my father. This was bad.

Jeanine dropped into a chair and began gnawing her fingernails. Tears were running down her cheeks. "What if he's...he's bleeding into his brain? He could be having a stroke."

"He's not having a stroke. You can't even talk if you're having a stroke." At least I didn't think you could. "It's just a concussion. People get concussions all the time. Connor got one last summer in Little League. He was totally knocked out, and a couple of days later he was fine."

"But this could be different. Dad could have ruptured an artery. Brain cells could be dying every second."

"Everything okay in there?" Dad called.

"Everything's fine," I called back.

"Hey, do you know what this ice is for?"

"Your head!" Jeanine and I both yelled.

"Oh, yeah. Thanks."

"See," wept Jeanine, snot boinging from her nose. "He's dying."

"He has a headache! He's not dying."

"How do you know?"

I didn't actually know. My best guess was that he wasn't dying, but the problem with Jeanine always acting like she knows everything is that sometimes you believe her. "So what do you want to do?"

"There's that clinic in town."

"How would we get there?"

"We could take the car."

"Dad can't drive like that!"

"Not Dad. You! It's not far, and it's basically a straight line."

"Are you crazy? I can't drive." Had Dad somehow also hit Jeanine's head on his way down?

"You can't get a license or anything, but you can drive. I've seen you play Speedway. You're a great driver."

"That's a video game! This is a real road with real cars."

"We're not talking about rush hour in Times Square. How many other cars will even be on the road?"

"Hello? Anybody there?" my father called from the living room.

This time Jeanine went. "Yeah, Dad. We're here."

"I have a nasty headache."

"Yeah, Dad. We know. You fell off the roof. Just keep the ice on."

Then she went to the front door, took my father's car keys from the hook, and put them on the table in front of me. "You really want to leave him there asking the same question every five minutes till Mom gets home?"

People get concussions all the time and don't die, but Jeanine had really freaked me out with all that stuff about ruptured arteries and brain cells dying.

"Okay, let's go, but I'm not taking the car."

"So, how are we getting there?"

"I have an idea."

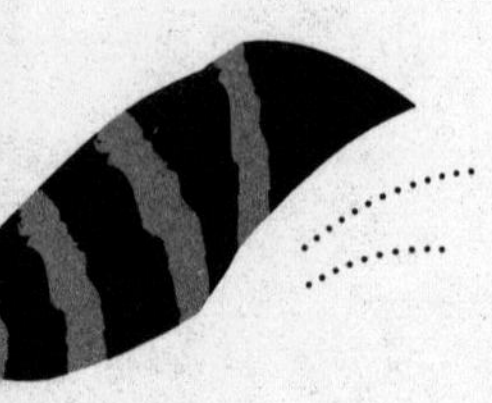

a minute, he forgot what he was doing and just quit pedaling. Luckily, he put his feet down before he tipped over too far.

"What if we just kept saying, 'You're riding a bike. You're riding a bike,' over and over?" I said.

Jeanine started back up the porch steps. "I'm getting the car keys."

"You are not! I told you, that's crazy and, like, against the law."

"So how are we getting there?"

"I have another idea. It's crazy too but not against the law."

"What?"

"What about the baby buggy?"

"For who?"

"Dad!" I called as I ran off to get it.

Behind the house, a big plastic sheet covered the brand-new, two-person bike. Nobody had even ridden it yet, but it was already set up with the baby buggy attached. I pulled off the sheet. The bike was so shiny that the blue paint looked silver. I flicked up the kickstand and wheeled it out front.

"Dad and I haven't even tried it out yet." Jeanine said.

"You ride it like a regular bike. I rode one with Mom in Montreal that time."

Jeanine studied the bike. "Maybe I could fit in the buggy with Dad."

"What are you talking about? Dad'll just barely fit in the buggy by himself. Plus, I can't pull both of you."

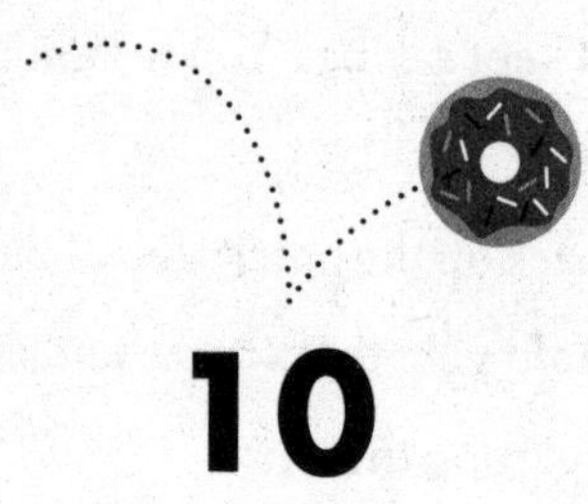

10

"Ooooooh, cake!" Dad said, grabbing one as we led him through the kitchen to the front door. "Mmm." Chocolate dribble down his chin. "Can we take some for the road?"

I thought concussions made people sick to their stomach, that didn't seem true in Dad's case. "Sure." I grabbed three m cakes and tied them up in a dish towel.

When we'd gotten Dad down the porch steps, I told Jear wait there. Then I ran around to the back of the house, gc bike, and wheeled it out front.

"What are you thinking? He can't bike like this," Jeani

"How do you know? Let's just see."

Dad got on fine. He even pedaled off okay, but aft

"Well, why does Dad need to go in the buggy at all? Why can't he ride on the second seat?"

"It's for a kid. Dad's legs are way too long. Besides, you saw him on the bike. After five minutes, he'll fall right off or just tip over and take us all down."

"Hey, guys?" Since his bike adventure, Dad had been sitting on the porch steps staring into space. "What's this for?" He held up the ice pack.

"Your head. You fell off the roof," I said.

"Why was I on the roof?"

"Because you're a nuddy," Jeanine said.

I poked her hard through her bathrobe.

"What? He's not going to remember in five minutes." She looked back at the bike and took a deep breath. "Oh, fine. We'll take him in the buggy." Then she snapped her fingers right in Dad's face. "C'mon. We're going. Get up!"

Dad looked confused but stood up.

I tied the dish towel around the remaining cake and put it in the baby buggy. "We'll have to walk down to the road."

"You heard him, walk!" Jeanine said, giving Dad a shove.

Again, Dad did as he was told, which just made me sad. I would have given anything right then to hear him go off in French at Jeanine for bossing him around.

When we started down Terror Mountain, I was leading the bike and Jeanine was leading Dad. But when we hit the first steep bit, the baby buggy swung downhill so fast, the bike ripped out of my hands and crashed into a tree. After that, Jeanine and Dad walked on either side of the buggy to keep it from veering into the woods. Jeanine kept reminding Dad to stay right up next to it, but of course, he kept forgetting, and before she could remind him again, he'd fall behind, and the buggy would skid off his side into a tree. Then the bike would stop suddenly, and the handlebars would smash into my chest.

"Dad!" I'd yell.

"Oh, was that me?" he'd say. Again.

It took forever, but we did finally make it to the bottom, and somehow, even with all the crashing into trees, I was pretty sure none of my ribs were broken, and we hadn't wrecked the bike or the buggy, though neither looked brand-new anymore.

"Okay, get in," I said when we'd wheeled the bike and buggy out onto the road.

"Where?" Dad said.

"Here." I held open the zippered flap on the buggy.

Dad snorted a laugh. "Absolutely not."

"It's the only way," Jeanine said.

"Why can't I bike?"

"Because…because…you just can't! Now get in. And put this on your head." Jeanine handed him back the ice pack.

Dad stuck out his lips just like Zoe does when my parents yell at her, but he held the ice to his head anyway and said, "Fine." Then he turned his back to the buggy and lowered himself into it, leaving his feet still out on the road.

"We need all of you in there," I said.

"What do you suggest I do with these?" he said, kicking his legs straight out.

"They fold, don't they? Fold them." I picked up his legs one by one and put them inside the buggy. "See, no problem."

"Oh, yeah. This is great." Dad rolled his eyes.

I'm not going to lie. It didn't look comfortable. And, for sure, if we hit a bump, his kneecap would give him a nosebleed, but at least all he had to do was sit there.

Jeanine and I were just about to get on the bike when I realized she was still wearing her bathrobe. "Take off the robe."

"But it's cold, and I only have on pj's."

"You'll warm up on the bike."

"I can't ride into town in pj's," she said, as if two kids on a tandem bike pulling their six-foot father in a baby buggy wouldn't give people enough to talk about.

"How is your bathrobe better than pj's?"

"It kind of looks like a coat. People won't be able to tell it's a robe."

"Uh, they will if they're not blind. Look, it could get caught. It's dangerous."

"Really?"

"Yes, really. Why don't you ever believe me about anything? I know I'm not a genius, but I'm not stupid. I do know *some* useful things."

"Fine." Jeanine took off the robe and stuffed it into the buggy. "It's freezing."

I put a leg over the bike and held it up while Jeanine climbed on behind me. Then I pushed off.

I was expecting to feel super wobbly at least at first, but the bike felt pretty balanced.

"I like this," Jeanine called from behind. "It's kind of fun."

Just then, the bike swerved, and I had to lean way out to keep it from falling over. "Jeanine!"

"Sorry. I was just trying to get more comfortable."

"Don't move. I mean, just move your legs. Not anything else."

Usually when I'm riding to town, I get on and just go. I don't even have to think about turning the pedals over. But this was different. This felt like work, and we weren't even on a hill yet.

Then I looked down and realized why I was working so hard. Jeanine's boots were going around, but when the pedals dropped, I could see the ground between the pedal and the boot. She wasn't pushing at all. Her feet were just along for the ride. "Jeanine! Pedal!"

"I am."

"No, you're not. Your feet are on a merry-go-round. They need to push. C'mon. Right. Left. Right. Left."

"But that's hard," she whined.

"It's called riding a bike." I stood up on the pedals.

"Why are you doing that?"

"You get more power like this. But just sit. It'll be too hard to balance with both of us standing."

When the road flattened out, I sat back down. My back was killing me, and I was breathing hard.

"Are we almost there?"

"Can you please just pedal?" I was too out of breath to talk.

Jeanine was quiet for a while after that, and she was definitely pushing the pedals down now because I could hear her puffing behind me.

"I don't like this!" she shouted as we started to pick up speed heading down a long hill.

"I can't do anything about gravity, Jeanine."

"Can't you slow us down?"

"We're not even going that fast. Just relax."

But Jeanine didn't relax. Instead, Jeanine did what Jeanine does. She freaked, and the bike began to dip and swerve like it was trying to shake me off.

"Okay! Okay!" I slowed us down until the screaming and the swooping stopped. "Better?"

"Better."

Since even with Jeanine actually pedaling, we had no chance of making it up the monster hill outside of town, I stopped at the bottom of it. I'd planned on picking Jeanine and Dad up at the traffic light at the top, but once he was out of the buggy, Dad swore he'd never get back in, so I rode all the way to the clinic and waited for them there.

"Hello? Anybody here?" Jeanine called as we entered the empty waiting room.

Besides some armchairs and a coffee table, it didn't look much like other waiting rooms I'd seen. The walls were crowded with colorful paintings from floor to ceiling, and there was no window with a receptionist sitting in it.

"Hey! Just come on up," a man's voice called.

"Up?" I called back.

It seemed weird to have a doctor's office on more than one floor. If someone were really sick, would you want to make them climb a flight of stairs?

"Yeah, come up!" the man said again.

"I'll go," I said and left Jeanine quizzing Dad on U.S. capitals in the waiting room. These he remembered perfectly, at least according to Jeanine. I couldn't tell you since I've taken a stand against memorizing facts readily available on the internet.

"Perfect timing. I need another pair of hands," I heard the man say as I climbed the stairs.

Was it possible that Petersville was so short on able bodies that the doctor let just anybody pitch in to help with surgical procedures? My stomach somersaulted like I was in an elevator coming down too fast. I'm not so good with blood, mine or anybody else's.

What I saw when I got up there did make me want to run back down again, but it wasn't some lady having a wart sawed off. It was a man, super thin, dripping with sweat and wearing way too little clothing to be inviting in visitors. The only thing separating him from complete nakedness were those teeny, tiny running shorts. You know the ones that are so small you're worried something will fall out? Those.

The man held a paintbrush in each hand, and he was going at an enormous canvas like he was trying to teach it a lesson. It must have been fighting back too, because the thick carpet of hair on his chest was more blue than gray.

Before I could ask where the doctor was, the guy was rushing at me, shoving a long piece of cardboard into my hands, and then pulling me by it back over to the painting. "Here, just hold it like this," he said, pressing it against the canvas at an angle.

"But—"

"Shush! Quiet!" he ordered, raising his paintbrush over his mouth so fast, he splattered both our faces with paint. Then he began painting furiously around the cardboard, covering not just the canvas but both my hands with cold, syrupy paint.

"But—"

"Shush!"

"It's just—"

"Please, please, please! This will only take one minute, sixty seconds, nothing."

Okay, sixty seconds is nothing, but it was so not sixty. I counted. Somewhere after 200 Mississippi, I let the cardboard drop.

"Oh no," he said, more sad than angry. "I was almost done."

"Look," I said. "I really need to find Dr. Charney."

"You're not Joe?"

"No."

"You're not here about the painting apprenticeship?"

"No, I'm here to see the doctor."

"Why didn't you say something?" he said, tossing his paintbrushes into a coffee can. I must have looked annoyed because then he said, "Kidding," and knocked me a little too hard on the shoulder with a blue fist. "Just give me a second."

This guy was the doctor? Maybe "doctor" meant something different in Petersville.

"Fever?" He went to a sink in the corner of the room and began washing his hands. "Flu's already making the rounds. Have you been vaccinated?"

He spoke Doctor at least. "Uh, no. It's not me. It's my dad. Downstairs. He fell off our roof. We think he has a concussion."

"I'm sure Dad's just fine, but let's go take a look," he said, drying his hands as he headed for the stairs.

"Um, aren't you forgetting something?" I tugged at my sweatshirt. Personally, I thought he could have used a shower too given all the paint and sweat, but the least he could do was put on some clothes.

"Right, back in a flash." He dashed behind a screen that hid a corner of the room. As I waited, I looked around the large, messy space, which, in addition to artist studio, was part kitchen, living room, office, and tool shop.

A minute later, he popped out from behind the screen in a white lab coat, tufts of blue chest hair peeking out above the collar. "Ready!"

I guess he thought, like the shower, a shirt was optional. I couldn't help wondering if he even had underwear on under there. Just the thought skeeved me out so much I couldn't look at him.

"I run hot," he said like he could hear what I was thinking.

"Oh," I said, and hurried down the stairs, trying not to think about whether what he'd just told me was, "No, I'm not wearing anything under this lab coat." It wasn't till I got to the bottom that I noticed he was still barefoot.

Not surprisingly, Jeanine insisted on interrogating Dr. Charney before she let him touch Dad. And I have to admit, it was one of those times that I was happy Jeanine is so Jeanine.

First, she demanded to know why Dr. Charney didn't have a receptionist like a real doctor. Was it because he didn't actually have any patients?

Not having a receptionist meant he could charge people less for seeing him, he explained. Then he picked up a date book from the coffee table and showed her how people came into the clinic and penciled in their own appointments. This actually seemed really smart to me. If it did to Jeanine too, she didn't let on.

Next, Jeanine wanted to know why Dr. Charney wasn't seeing patients that day, a weekday.

Because, he explained, he took Thursdays off and saw patients on Saturdays so they wouldn't have to take off work.

"What a great idea!" Dad said.

Jeanine was still not satisfied.

Finally, Jeanine asked about the doctor's school degrees. Dr.

Barber, our pediatrician, had a wall in his waiting room covered with framed degrees and covers of magazines that named him one of the best doctors in New York City. "Where are yours?" she asked.

Dr. Charney screwed up his mouth, then walked out of the waiting room.

Jeanine and I exchanged looks. Was he coming back? Was this the question fast-talking Dr. Charney didn't have an answer to? This wasn't entirely good news since an artist pretending to be a doctor was still better than no doctor at all. I was just beginning to wonder what we should do now when Dr. Charney marched back in, two yellowed sheets of paper held high. "Found them!" he said with a big smile and handed them to Jeanine.

Her eyes bulged.

"Happy now?" he said.

"You went to Yale? Did you know that five U.S. Presidents went to Yale?"

"I am aware," Dr. Charney said.

"So why don't you have these out here on the wall where people can see them?"

He held up the papers and studied them. "Not really much to look at, are they? Besides, then there would be less room for these," he said, pointing to his paintings.

By the time Dr. Charney was finally permitted to examine him, my father had started to get his memory back. He could now remember that we'd told him he'd fallen off the roof, which seemed like a good sign even if he couldn't remember the fall itself. Either way, Dr. C was sure he hadn't had a stroke. Just to be safe though, he wanted Mom to take him for a CAT scan. So when she and Zoe finally got to Petersville an hour after we'd called her from the doctor's office, she had to turn around and drive right back to Crellin with Dad. Josh's mom said we could stay with her and Josh at the library till they got back.

The first thing Jeanine did when we got to the library was sit down at the computer and google Dr. Z. Charney. There were so many hits, I was sure they couldn't all be him. The first was an Amazon link. Jeanine clicked on it.

A photo of a smiling man holding a book called *Hometown Healing: Breaking All the Rules* popped up. He was wearing way more clothing than I would have bet the man I'd just met would ever wear—shirt, tie, and blazer—but there was no denying it was him. Under the photo, it said the book was about being a doctor in small towns where most people don't have much money and few have health insurance. It also said that the author had practiced medicine in small towns all over the country before settling in Petersville, New York.

The next hits were all articles about the book and the awards it had won. About halfway down the first page though, the results changed. They weren't about Dr. Z. Charney anymore, but someone named Zed Charney, painter.

"No way," I said. "Find a photo."

It took some clicking, but there, on some art gallery site in a photo of a party celebrating his new exhibition in Seattle was Dr. C, wearing a shirt open to his belly button, the chest hair I was becoming way too familiar with out there for everyone with an internet connection to see.

"Mom told me that this new museum in Spain just bought two of his paintings," said Josh, who'd joined us at the computer.

I couldn't remember seeing Jeanine so impressed by anyone living since she'd learned about some kid who'd figured out that the federal government could save millions of dollars each year if it just changed the font it used when it printed stuff.

I was blown away too. I'd never met someone like Dr. C, not just someone who'd done as much as he had, but someone who'd done all that stuff and didn't even go around telling everyone he had.

By the rules Zane Kramer, and now Charlie too, believed the world worked, Dr. Charney simply couldn't exist. What he'd done, who he was, none of it was possible.

But it was. And Dr. C was living, breathing proof.

"Hey, what's that?" Josh said, pointing to the dish towel sack I was still carrying around.

"Oh, right." I'd completely forgotten. There was still one cake left, so I told Josh it was something I owed Winnie and I'd explain after I went to the General Store to give it to her.

"What's this?" Winnie said when I untied the dish towel and set the cake on the counter. "Looks like somebody put their fist through it."

"We had some bike trouble. It'll still taste good. Do you have a microwave so we can zap it for a few seconds? It's better warm."

"Radiation makes it tastes better? How 'bout mercury? That make it taste better too? Maybe I have some asbestos we could shake over it like powdered sugar?"

"Never mind," I said. It would still taste good. The chocolate center just wouldn't pack the same ooze. Her loss.

Winnie leaned over and sniffed. "What is it anyway?"

"Molten chocolate cake."

"Just chocolate, right? I don't like it when people get all fancy and mix the chocolate up with stuff that's got no business with chocolate. Some guy came in here trying to sell me chocolate bars with chili peppers in them. What's that about?"

Clearly I was getting points for chocolate. That was something at least.

"I know," I said. "My parents took us to this fancy restaurant once that put lavender in the chocolate mousse. It was like eating that dried stuff people use to make clothes smell good."

"Potpourri in chocolate? An abomination, that's what that is."

I didn't know what an abomination was, but she seemed to be agreeing with me, which felt like a good sign. "Yeah, don't worry. This is just chocolate and eggs and butter and sugar. It's my mom's famous recipe."

"Famous, huh? Did they write about it in the papers?" She pointed to the frame on the counter.

"I just meant people love it." How was it that every other word out of my mouth got her all worked up? Worked up wasn't a good way to go into a taste test.

"Well, I'm not everyone," she muttered as she disappeared into the back of the store. Moments later, she was back, fork in hand. "Just chocolate, right?" She jabbed the cake like she was trying to wake it up.

"Just chocolate, I promise."

"Okay, here we go..."

I tried to read her face as she chewed.

"Didn't anybody ever tell you it's rude to watch a person eat?"

"Sorry." I turned around and pretended to study the egg cartons.

"Hmn," she grunted.

I snuck a quick look just in time to see her take another bite, much bigger than the first.

"Not earth-shattering or anything," she said, still chewing, "but you should be able to make my doughnuts okay."

"Yes!" I spun around to face her.

"Not so fast," she said, wagging her fork at me. "Before you get that recipe, we need to hammer out the details. You bring your business plan?"

"You never told me I needed a business plan."

"I never told you not to put chili peppers in chocolate cake either, but you knew that. Of course you need a business plan. You're selling something, right? If you're selling, you're in business. You need a budget. You need to figure out your costs. You need to figure out how many doughnuts you're planning to sell each day. I wouldn't recommend making more than forty for starters, no matter how much people beg. And then..."

I wanted to cry. I just wanted a chocolate cream doughnut. Now I was starting a business? I'd only come up with the idea to sell the doughnuts to get Winnie to give me the recipe and get my parents off my back.

"After all, I need to know your profits so I can figure out my cut," Winnie was saying when I started listening again.

"What? You want money? But I'm going to be doing all the work."

"But it's *my* recipe. They call it intellectual property. You've got to pay for a license to use what I created. Now that sounds fair, doesn't it?" She took another big bite of cake. She seemed quite pleased with how things were going. Why wouldn't she be? She'd gotten the stupid new kid in town to make her chocolate cake, and now she thought she was going to get him to pay her for the privilege of making her doughnuts.

"When you use a recipe from a cookbook, you don't have to buy a license," I argued.

"Ah, but you do," she said, dotting an *I* in the air with her fork. "You had to buy the cookbook."

Unfortunately, I could see her point. "How much do you want?"

"I told you. I can't figure that out without seeing the numbers."

"But I don't know anything about making a budget and all that other stuff. It sounds like a lot of math. Maybe I could get my sister to work on it. She's really good at that kind of thing."

"What are you talking about? This isn't math. It's common sense. Besides, this is *your* business. Why do you want to hand over the details of *your* business to just anybody?"

"She's not anybody. She's my sister."

"Even worse. Family members don't respect each other's property. It's the first rule of family: what's mine is yours. You really want somebody who can't tell the difference between yours and theirs working on your business?"

"She did sell my stuff at this tag sale we had once," I admitted.

"Of course she did! Family. They sell your stuff right out from under you."

"But I wouldn't even know how to start putting a budget together."

"Like I said, this isn't rocket science. Go across the street."

"What's across the street?"

"You have your sister do your reading for you too? Ever heard of a library?" she said, knocking on my head.

"You want me to do research?" I groaned. Those doughnuts were slipping farther away every second.

"Just tell Mary what you're looking for, and she'll point you in the right direction."

"I can't believe this," I muttered as I dragged myself out of the store.

"What was that?" Winnie called.

"Bye!" I shouted over my shoulder.

My only hope was that if I acted really stupid, Josh's mom would just do the budget for me. She was a librarian so she had to be pretty smart, and she wasn't family so I figured I could trust her more than Jeanine.

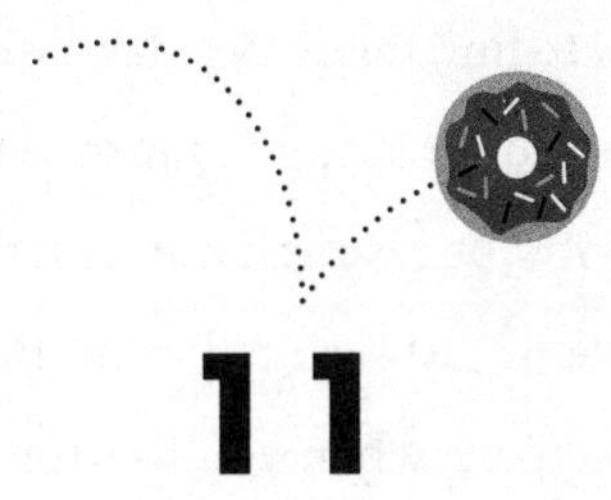

11

If you're ever thinking about starting your own business, you should really check out *Starting Your Own Business for Dummies*. It was definitely the most useful book Josh gave me. He was the one who helped me at the library that day, not his mom. She'd been too busy trying to keep Zoe from ripping out some little girl's pigtails. I hadn't been there when the fight broke out, but Josh told me later that it started when this girl said all fairies were made up except for the Tooth Fairy, who was obviously real because she had a job and money.

The truth is, I hadn't wanted to tell Josh about the doughnut business. So what if he loved Winnie's doughnuts? Wouldn't he think I was a weirdo for trying to build a business around something I'd never even tasted? Or maybe he'd think what

Charlie and his dad did, that kids can't start businesses at all, and that I was stupid to even try? But I needed those books, and I was sure he'd know how to find them. Besides, he'd find out eventually.

"Can I help?" he said the second I finished telling him about my project. "Not just with the research but with the actual business?"

I couldn't believe it. Josh wanted in on the doughnut stand. I guess that's what happens when you live someplace with so little entertainment. You're willing to try anything. Since he wasn't family, I said yes.

By the time my parents showed up at the library to take us home that day, Josh had found me a stack of books and flagged the ones he thought would be most useful. *Starting Your Own Business for Dummies* was on top.

"That doesn't mean I think you're stupid or anything, you know," Josh said as he handed me the books.

"Yeah, I know," I said, though I liked that he was the kind of person who'd check to make sure.

A few days later, I woke up and my window was frosted over with ice crystals. Outside, the grass was frozen stiff and crackled when you walked on it. Since it was only November, I figured it would warm up again, at least a little, but it never did. And before I knew it, the pond was frozen. Josh said we'd gotten "lucky" winter had come early because it meant a longer skating season. I told him that now when I biked to town, the cold made my nose run and then froze the snot to my face. I didn't feel "lucky" that winter had come early, but I promised to give pond skating a try anyway.

I can now tell you from personal experience, Dad was wrong. Pond skating *is* almost as boring as regular skating. I say "almost" because the possibility that you might fall through the ice at any second does add a certain something. It didn't matter that my parents had it tested. First of all, the guy who tested it wasn't actually a professional ice tester. He was Jim the Kidnapper, also known as Jim, the carpenter my parents hired to work on the roof since Dad wasn't allowed up there anymore. Second, there was no magic test. He just drilled a hole in the ice, stuck a stick down into it, pulled it out, and said, "Should be fine. But get off if you hear any cracking."

I never would have risked my life just to skate around in circles, but it turns out skating is actually not at all boring if you can whack something across the ice with a stick at the same time.

When Josh first came over with his hockey stuff, I was the worst anyone has ever been at anything. I spent the whole day crawling around the ice, using my body to block the puck. But after only a week, I could skate and flick the puck with my stick at the same time, at least when I didn't accidently skate right past it. It took me so long to stop and change direction, by the time I got back to where it had been, Josh had already whisked it off to the other side of the pond.

Josh was amazing, better than I was at basketball, better than anyone my age was at any sport, at least that I'd seen in real life. It was as if he'd been born on ice skates. He could run and spin and glide. He could dance, bits of ice spraying out from his blades with each new move. He zoomed backward and forward, dodging and weaving between invisible players charging at him for the puck.

Josh said I might be able to make the rec team if I could get my hockey stop and backward skating down. I was pretty sure rec was just a nice way of saying the worst, but I didn't care as long as I'd get to play.

Zoe wanted to learn to skate, but she was too scared. Every time Josh and I went down to the pond, she'd put on her water wings, snowsuit, and skates and just sit in a pile of leaves at the edge of the pond throwing rocks onto the ice. It was Josh who finally got her to get on.

That day, he and I were doing this drill he'd taught me where you go back and forth across the pond skating as fast as you can, hockey stopping on each end, until you're so tired you can't move.

I couldn't go fast or stop fast, so it took me forever to get from one side to the other. It also took a lot of concentration since I was so bad I had to tell my legs and feet exactly what to do every second: *push, push, straighten, turn, bend.* I was so focused I didn't even notice when Josh stopped flying past me every thirty seconds.

I have no idea what he said or how long it took him to get Zoe to take that first step onto the ice, but by the time I realized Josh wasn't doing the drill anymore, he had her way out in the middle of the pond, skating between his legs, and she didn't even look scared. She had a huge smile on her face.

"Yay, Zoe!" I yelled.

She smiled even bigger.

"Hey! Can you bring us one of those?" Josh called, pointing to the circle of plastic chairs my parents had set up next to the pond.

"Onto the ice?"

"Uh-huh."

Zoe clearly wasn't the first kid Josh had taught to skate. The chair was genius. Zoe could lean on it and push it along the ice. By the time we went inside, she was pushing off and gliding a good ways holding on to the chair with just one hand.

When we got back to the house, we went straight to the living room to warm up by the fire. Jeanine was in there on the couch reading *The Wolves of Willoughby Chase.* Again. I'm pretty sure she was still staying up at night reading it because her eyes were puffy and red all the time. If you asked my parents, this was from allergies even though we all knew Jeanine stopped getting allergies when it got cold.

Jeanine hadn't gotten on the ice even once and not just because she was convinced she was going to fall through it. Now that she was done with gathering stuff for her project, she never left the house. At least before, she'd go outside to collect leaves and dirt and "scat," which is what she called the animal poop she picked up with rubber gloves, put in ziplock bags, and stored in our freezer. But now that she had everything she needed, she wouldn't even get off the couch. She sat there all day long working on her project and studying for the Regional Solve-a-Thon, this huge competition for all the Jeanine Levins and Kevin Metzes in the Northeast who want to see how many math problems they can do in six hours. When she needed a break, she'd read *The Wolves of Willoughby Chase* for the bazillionth time.

I took off my jacket and gloves and hung them on the fireplace screen. "I'm making hot chocolate. Who wants?"

"Is this a trick question?" Josh said.

"With marshandyellows," Zoe said.

"Me too," Jeanine said, without looking up from the book.

"What's hot chocolate without marshandyellows?" Josh said

and plopped down on the couch next to Jeanine. "You know, *The Wolves of Willoughby Chase* is, like, one of my top favorite books of all time."

Jeanine sat up. "*You've* read *The Wolves of Willoughby Chase*?"

"Only like a hundred times."

"Me too!"

I felt like someone had just punched me in the stomach.

Zoe tugged on my hand. "Hot chocolate!" I was standing at the entrance to the living room watching Jeanine and Josh like they were behind glass. "Now," she said, pulling me into the kitchen.

As I stirred the milk in the saucepan, I listened to Josh and Jeanine talking in the living room.

Jeanine: "Have you read the sequel?"

Josh: "*Black Hearts in Battersea*? Yeah, not as good."

Jeanine: "I *know*. Um, do you think you'd want to join a book club with me and my friend Kevin? He lives in Manhattan, but he'll join by Skype."

Josh: "Sure. That sounds cool. My mom can get us the books on interlibrary loan if you want."

Jeanine: "Oh, yeah."

My skin felt prickly all over. "Hot chocolate!" I yelled. The milk was barely hot, but I poured it into the cups anyway. I stirred and stirred, but the cocoa clumped up and wouldn't dissolve.

"So I'm joining your book club," Josh said as he and Jeanine came into the kitchen.

Jeanine laughed. "Tris doesn't do book clubs. He isn't really a reader." Then she picked up her hot chocolate and took a sip. "Uch, this is cold," she said and went back into the living room.

Josh, Zoe, and I sat down at the kitchen table and drank our awful hot chocolate.

"Thanks for the making this," Josh said.

"I took the milk off too soon."

"It's still good."

I shrugged.

"The marshandyellows are good," Zoe said.

"Great," I said.

She put her cup down and squinted at me. "How come you have the mad face?"

"I'm not mad."

"You have the face." She stuck out her chin and mashed her lips together.

"*Are* you mad?" Josh asked.

"No, I'm just...don't worry about it."

What could I say? Don't be so nice? You can't be in my sister's book club? He'd think I was a complete jerk.

Besides, I wasn't mad at him. This wasn't his fault. It was

Jeanine's. Had I ever asked Kevin to play basketball? There were rules about sisters and brothers and friends, and Jeanine had broken them. Josh wasn't the only kid in Petersville. If she wanted a friend here, she should leave the house and find one.

Thanksgiving has always been my favorite holiday. Basically, because it's all about food and being thankful that you have food, which, not to brag, I feel like I am normally anyway. Not because I think so much more about world hunger than the next kid, but because I think way more about food than the next kid. Anyway, since food is food no matter where you are, and since Mom's food is always amazing, I figured Thanksgiving could be the way it was supposed to be even in Petersville.

Then Charlie called.

It was after dinner. We were in the middle of dessert, something new Mom was calling Three P Crumble because it's made with pears, plums, and pecans. We were arguing about whether it was good enough to make the menu. I was a big no. She'd left the skins on the plums, and they'd made the whole thing bitter.

Suddenly, the lights went out.

We thought it was the power, but then the phone rang. I knew it was Charlie calling to ask what he should bring since Thanksgiving was only a week away.

I jumped up and felt my way to the living room. Somewhere in there, my foot caught something and brought it down with a crash.

"Sorry!" I yelled as I patted down the couch for the phone. I was pretty sure I'd just destroyed a half-built, motorized bird feeder, Dad's latest project.

"Hello?"

I was right. It was Charlie.

All the things I'd been dying to tell him about flooded my brain: Josh, the Purple Demon, the flash flood, ice hockey…

"Hey! So, it's like the North Pole up here, and my room's in the attic, which is extra cold so bring all the clothes you own," I said, speaking as fast as Josh. "And definitely bring a sleeping bag because mine smells funny since Zoe used it and—"

"We're not coming," Charlie said. "I know. It sucks."

"Why? What happened?"

"Nothing. Or, I mean, not just one thing. Justin's got this cold, and my dad's been working really hard. Oh, plus my mom says they didn't know it was so far when they said yes."

What? Nobody had gotten hit by a bus? Nobody had bird flu?

I was getting the dog-ate-my-homework, this-seat-is-saved, didn't-you-get-the-invitation. And not just from anybody. From Charlie.

The Kramers didn't want to come. Fine. They and my parents were just friends because Charlie and I had been forever. But what about Charlie? I knew what angry Charlie sounded like—spitting, cursing, I'll-show-them Charlie. This wasn't him.

"It's not like you won't be coming back to the city, right?" he said. "I mean *everybody* comes to the city sometime."

"I guess," I said, wondering what Charlie would say if I told him Josh had never been to New York City.

"My mom says it will just be easier to see you on your trips back home."

"Back home, huh?" I said.

"What?"

He didn't get it. "Nothing."

"And she said maybe we can go up there in the summer. You know, when it's not so cold."

"Sure." Sure, summer, seven months from now.

Then we both went quiet, which feels weird when you're on the phone, because you can't see the other person, and you start to feel like you're alone, especially when you're standing there in the dark thinking about the things you wanted to say but suddenly don't anymore.

Then Charlie said, "Anyway, I got to go. Sam and I are going back to school. They're keeping the gym open late so we can get a little more practice in before tomorrow."

He wasn't coming for Thanksgiving. He hadn't asked me anything about Petersville, and now he was getting off?

"Oh, right, tryouts," I said, and as I did, I could feel this dark corner of me hope he wouldn't make the team.

"Let me know when you're coming home," he said, and it felt even worse this time than it had the first time he'd said it.

Mom and Dad did their best to cheer me up. Mom promised to make all my favorite dishes, including double-layer carrot cake with coconut frosting and baby brussels sprouts with pancetta (think bacon but better). Then she and Dad came up with this really "fun" idea to make Thanksgiving even more special: we were going to pick our own turkey, not plucked and headless from a butcher, but live with feathers from a farm.

I think they thought it was going to be like picking your own Christmas tree, not that any of us had ever done that before either. The thing about a Christmas tree though is that even if you're chopping one down, it's a plant, so it's pretty easy to get over the whole ending-a-life thing. Turkeys, however, are very obviously alive. They don't actually "gobble, gobble," and they're not cute or anything, but they do make noise and run around. Another important difference between Christmas trees and turkeys: we don't keep Christmas trees in little jails where they walk around looking sad and begging to be rescued.

So, let's just say, this was one more "surprise" that would have been perfect for that other family, the one with the four-year-old girl who loves staring at sad turkeys in little jails, because that girl wouldn't have masterminded the biggest turkey breakout in Thunder Hill Farm pick-your-own-turkey history.

Luckily, turkeys aren't very smart—how much brain could fit into those tiny heads anyway?—so even with Zoe chasing them out of their cells, yelling, "Run! Run!" they refused to go very far.

I'd been afraid Mr. Jennings, the guy who owned the farm, would flip out, which particularly worried me because he was the size and shape of a WWF wrestler. But he just laughed. He wouldn't even let Mom and Dad make it up to him by buying the biggest, most expensive turkey he had.

The worst part about my parents' stupid idea was that when Thanksgiving did finally come, and Mom had made this amazing dinner and brought out that delicious turkey, I couldn't eat it. Not one bite. I kept seeing all those birds running around Mr. Jennings's yard, and I just couldn't separate the live birds running around in my head from the bird on our table. And the idea of putting one bite in my mouth was just impossible, like eating something that wasn't even food, like sand or a pencil or a sister. I tried to talk myself out of it. I tried so hard, but nothing worked. The thing that really drove me crazy: I was the only one who felt this way. Even

Zoe, the great turkey rescuer, ate three portions. Of course, they all said it was the best turkey ever.

Nobody got to eat dessert that night though because before Mom made it, all the lights went out again, just like they had when Charlie called. Dad offered to hold a flashlight while Mom made crepes—they're his favorite—but she didn't think it was a good idea. The lights came back on again sometime in the middle of the night but then went out again the next day, so my parents called an electrician. Of course, when he came, the lights worked just fine.

My parents have now hired every electrician in the county, but nobody has been able to figure out why, every few days, all the lights in the house turn off and refuse, no matter how nicely you ask, to turn back on. What really stumps people is that even when the lights go out, everything else works just fine. I told my parents to stop wasting their money, but they refuse to accept what I think is pretty obvious: when the Purple Demon gets bored, she turns out all the lights so she can watch us bump into things.

The Tuesday after Thanksgiving, I got an email from Charlie. The second I saw it in my inbox, that bad feeling I'd been carrying around since our call was suddenly gone because I knew what the email was going to say: sorry I couldn't come for Thanksgiving; sorry I didn't seem sorry; sorry I got off so fast; sorry I didn't ask one thing about Petersville; sorry about not sending more emails.

Then I clicked it open.

To: JaxTLevin441@mar.com

From: CKramerRocks@mar.com

Subject: Hey

I MADE IT!!

And that was it.

I wish I could tell you I sent an email right back and that it said: YAY!!!!!!!!!!!!! That's what the twelve-year-old kid in that other family, the one I was supposed to be, would have done right after he'd dug up worms in the backyard and made bark tea. But I didn't. Me, I stole *The Wolves of Willoughby Chase* off the couch where Jeanine had left it, climbed up to the attic, and stayed there in bed under the covers reading for the rest of the day.

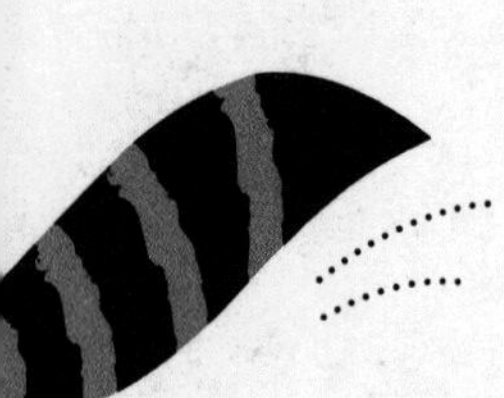

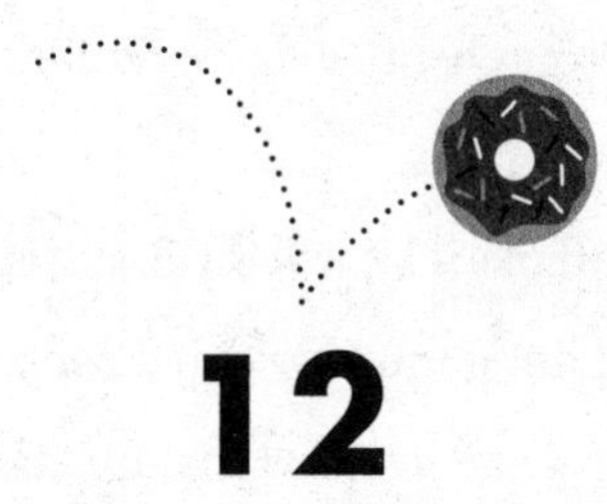

12

After I finished *Starting Your Own Business for Dummies,* I went back to the General Store to show Winnie the chapter on costs, because it was clear I'd need to know the doughnuts' ingredients to figure out what it would cost to make them. I was prepared for her to give me a hard time as usual, but instead she acted like she'd known all along I'd need the ingredients to put together the budget. She even said, "It's about time, Slick." She'd started calling me Slick by then. I never asked why, but I'm guessing it's because I'm not, so she thought it was a big laugh.

The next day, I got up early and shut myself in my parents' office with everything I'd need to work up the budget: the list of ingredients, *Starting Your Own Business for Dummies,* and a stack of Mom's peanut butter–butterscotch granola bars. The book says setting goals and sticking to them is key to getting your business off the ground, so I told myself I couldn't come out until I figured out how much of each ingredient we'd have to order every month.

Things started off okay. I knew my first step was just to come up with the number of doughnuts we'd make in a month. After talking to Winnie, Josh and I had decided that for starters, we'd sell eighty doughnuts every week: forty on Saturday and forty on Sunday. To get the number of doughnuts we'd sell in a month, I just had to multiply the eighty doughnuts we'd be making in a week times the number of weeks in a month:

$$80 \times 4 = 320$$

The next part wasn't too hard either. Since Winnie's recipe made ten doughnuts, all I had to do was to figure out how many batches of doughnuts I'd have to make to get 320 of them:

$$10 \times ? = 320$$

In fourth grade, Mr. Gratz taught us that if you have a times problem and you're looking for what to times your number by, you actually need to divide:

$$? = 320 \div 10$$

$$? = 32$$

This is where the problems started.

Problem number one: the list of ingredients was full of annoying fractions. They were all over the place—*3¾* cups of flour, *1⅓* cups of sugar, ¼ teaspoon of cinnamon. There were so many fractions I was sure Winnie had put them in there on purpose just to make the math harder.

Problem number two: I wasn't sure how to multiply fractions using the calculator on my parents' computer. Was I supposed to turn them into decimals and then multiply them? In the end, I just decided to do the calculations on paper, which took forever.

Problem number three: I knew I was making mistakes, like always. The thing is, all those other times I'd messed up some math problem, it had been in school, and those mistakes hadn't really mattered since those questions were all made-up. But *this* problem, the doughnut problem, wasn't made-up, and if I messed up this time, I'd be messing up something real.

Problem number four: because I was sure I was making mistakes, I kept redoing the problems. And the more worried I got, the more mistakes I made. And every time I redid a problem, I came out with a different answer, sometimes a really different answer.

Eventually, I'd erased and rewritten stuff so many times, I tore the paper. That's when I threw my pencil at the wall. And then, because that didn't make me feel any better, I threw a whole bunch of stuff at the wall: a tape dispenser, a plastic cup, a box of paper clips.

I was not in a good way, as Mom likes to say. I needed a break. I was out of granola bars. I'd missed lunch. I needed to eat and go outside and skate so fast I couldn't think about anything but moving and breathing.

But what about my goal? I'd set a goal, and the book said I needed to stick to it.

Then it came to me. I'd just set a new goal. Something easy. Something fast. The book never said you couldn't *change* goals. I looked back at the recipe.

Cocoa: 3 tablespoons. Three was a nice round number. Perfect. I'd figure out how many tablespoons of cocoa I'd need to make 320 doughnuts, come up with how many boxes of cocoa that was, and then I'd take a break.

3 tablespoons x 32 batches = 96 tablespoons

But how many boxes of cocoa was that? I slid the rolly chair across the floor to the computer.

"How many tablespoons are in a box of cocoa powder," I typed into Google and hit Return.

I crossed my fingers as I read through the results. There it was—fourth from the top. "There are thirty-five tablespoons in one eight-ounce carton of cocoa powder."

I rolled back across the desk and wrote:

8 oz. box of cocoa = 35 tablespoons

This was like the problem I'd done to figure out how many batches of doughnuts I'd need to make to get 320 doughnuts, only instead of batches I was looking for boxes.

? boxes x 35 tablespoons = 96 tablespoons

? = 96 ÷ 35

? = 2 with 26 left over

Since I couldn't buy part of a box, I'd have to round up.

Finally, I could fill in a square on the order sheet I'd made. Under *Cocoa,* I wrote: three boxes.

Done. I'd reached my new and improved (easier) goal. It was definitely break time.

Down in the kitchen, something sweet-and-spicy smelling was

cooking on the stove. I was so hungry, I didn't care enough to ask what it was. I just spooned out a big bowl and ate it standing up.

Then I grabbed my skates and ran out the door without even putting on a jacket or gloves.

When I got on the pond, I didn't practice hockey stops or skating backward. I just skated as fast as I could. In circles. Without thinking. And it wasn't boring. It was awesome. And when my legs burned and my ears stung and my fingers were numb and I couldn't take it anymore, I went back inside.

I actually couldn't wait to get back to work, maybe because now I had a plan. I'd get the budget done one small goal at a time. As I ran up the stairs, I decided I'd tackle the butter next.

Then I got to the office, and all that good feeling zapped right out of me.

Jeanine was in there. She had the budget in one hand and a red pencil in the other. "I think if you turned the mixed numbers into improper fractions, you'd make fewer mistakes," she said as she crossed something out.

My face, which had been freezing only a second before, suddenly felt like it was on fire. I ripped the paper out from under her pencil, making a big red slash across it.

"Hey! I'm not done. You know how many mistakes there are in there?" she said.

"I don't care!"

"You don't care?"

"I mean..." I was so mad, it was hard to speak. "I wasn't finished. I haven't...checked it over yet."

"Why don't you just let me do it?"

"Because..." I started, but then nothing else came out. I couldn't think of what I wanted to say or how to say it in a way that wouldn't make me feel even worse.

I grabbed the back of the rolly chair with both hands and tipped it forward till it dumped Jeanine off. Then I started pushing her out into the hall.

"Ow! You're hurting me," she said, shoving me back.

"Then get out!"

The next second, Mom was at the door, breathing like she'd run up the stairs. "What's going on here?"

"You need to tell Jeanine to get her own life. Maybe she could start by leaving the house for once."

"I was just trying to help. You *need* help. Look at all these mistakes." Jeanine grabbed the budget and shook it in my mother's face.

"I told you I wasn't done!"

Mom stepped between us, took the budget from Jeanine, and handed it back to me. "That's enough. Jeanine, go downstairs."

"But—"

"Now!"

Jeanine made a face and stormed out.

I crumpled the budget into a ball and threw it after her.

Mom looked at the ball of paper, then back at me. "Don't you need that?"

"You heard her. It's all wrong."

"She didn't say it was *all* wrong." She picked up the paper and smoothed it out on the desk. "Here, get back to work, and I'll send Zoe up with some snickerdoodles in a bit."

"I don't feel like working on it anymore." I dropped into the chair and looked at all the crossed-out numbers. "Maybe I *should* just let her do it."

Mom frowned. "Is that what you want?"

Part of me did. The part that just wanted it done. And done by someone who wouldn't make mistakes. But then, there was the other part of me that didn't. And not just because Winnie told me I couldn't trust family or even because it would feel like cheating. It was more than that.

"Everything's so easy for her."

"Everything?" Mom looked at me hard.

I shrugged. That's what it felt like. I didn't care if it were true.

Mom put her hands on my shoulders and squeezed. "I got you something. I was going to wait till you got the whole recipe, but I don't know, now seems like the right time." She left the room and came back a few minutes later with a cardboard box that she put down in front of me on the desk.

I picked up a pair of scissors, sliced open the box, and looked inside. Whatever was in there was covered in so much Bubble Wrap, I couldn't even guess what it was.

"So?" she said as I uncovered the final layer.

"What is it?" I didn't have the first clue what the thing in my hands was. It looked like something you'd use to give a giant a flu shot.

"It's for the doughnuts. To stuff them. It's a pastry gun. See, you fill it with cream here." She unscrewed the back. "Then you shoot the cream out the tip. It'll be way easier to use than those bags." Mom uses special bags with metal tips for filling stuff like cream puffs, but they have to be twisted and squeezed in just the right way.

I picked up the gun, squeezed the plunger, and imagined a stream of chocolate cream flying out of it.

"So cool, right?" she said, her eyes all big like she was looking at the world's first time machine and not just a tool for cramming gooey stuff into baked goods.

"So cool. Thanks. When did you get this?"

"A while ago. When you told me about the project."

"But how did you know I was going to… I mean, I don't even have the recipe yet."

"Yeah, but I know you. You'll get it." She was smiling her big smile, the one that shows her crooked tooth. "And now you really have to get it, right? I mean, you kinda *owe* me now since I shelled out for the gun." She crossed her arms and squeezed her lips together like she was suddenly all serious.

"Okay, okay. But *only* because you got me the pastry gun."

"All right, then get back to work!" She smiled again. "I'll send Zo Zo up with the cookies soon."

I worked straight through the afternoon, took a break for dinner, and then went back to work. It was past midnight by the time I crawled into bed, but I'd filled in every box on the order form. I'd stuck to the plan, one small goal at a time. Then I'd triple-checked my work, and this time, I got the same answers. I knew there were probably a few wrong numbers, but they were *my* wrong numbers. So I was okay with them because it meant the right ones were mine too, and that felt better than not having any wrong numbers ever would.

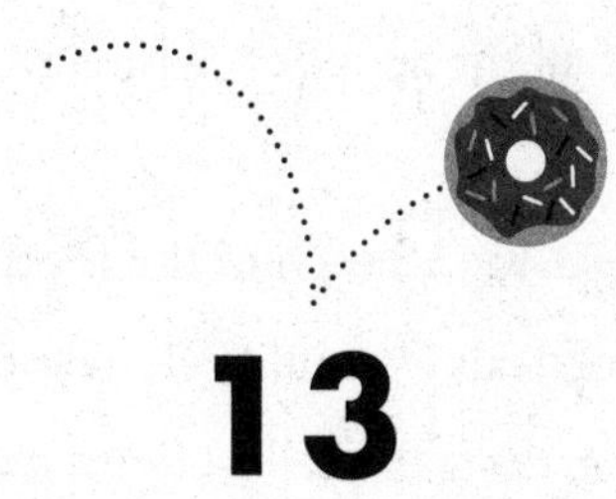

13

Starting Your Own Business for Dummies said if you were opening a restaurant or café, you should buy your ingredients wholesale. I had no idea what that meant, but one great thing about a book for dummies is that it assumes you don't know anything about anything. What's great about that too is when you already know something the book thinks you don't, you feel kind of smart.

The gist of wholesale is actually simple. If you're buying stuff for your business, other businesses cut you a deal on price. We got to buy our ingredients wholesale because we needed them for our doughnut business.

Josh was actually the one who came up with the list of food suppliers who offered what we needed wholesale. Poking around on the internet, he'd found this food supplier site where you type in your location and the foods you want, press Enter, and presto! It spits out a list of all the suppliers who have what you need and deliver to your area.

The next step was to call each of the food suppliers on the list and see what kind of deals we could get. Between figuring out what to say and actually making the calls, I figured it would take us a full day. Since most of the suppliers only worked Monday to Friday, we decided to do it on a Monday that Josh had off from school.

I was still eating breakfast when I heard Josh's mom's car coming up the driveway that morning. Mom was hunched over some papers opposite me, and Zoe was playing with pans on the kitchen floor.

Josh knocked, then opened the door and peeked inside. "Okay to come in?"

"Yup," I said through a mouthful of oatmeal. "Almost done."

"Hi, Josh," Mom said without looking up.

"Hi."

"Welcome to Zoe's Purple Giraffe!" Zoe said as she stirred a pan of ice cubes with a wooden spoon.

"What's Zoe's Purple Giraffe?" Josh asked and not in a you're-so-weird kind of way, but like he actually wanted to know and was talking to a real person.

"My restaurant," Zoe answered, stirring so hard ice cubes flew out of the bowl and across the floor.

Josh looked around the room as if he were seeing it for the first time. "Cozy. I like it."

Zoe sipped from the spoon and made a face. "Too much salt! Hand me the bear!" She pointed to the honey bear on the floor next to Josh's foot.

Josh gave her the bear, and she squeezed a long ribbon into the bowl. Then she put her head back and squeezed an even longer one straight into her mouth.

Josh laughed.

"Mom?" I said.

"What?"

"Do you see what's going on here?"

"She's playing. It's fine." She stood up. "Look, can you guys watch her for a bit? I have to go upstairs to talk to Dad about something."

"Mom, please. This is the one day Josh has to call food suppliers."

"It will only take a second."

"Sure," Josh said to my mother. "Really. It's fine," he said to me.

"Thanks so much. Just fifteen minutes."

"Fifteen minutes? Didn't you just say, 'a second'?" I said.

"Oh, and I had an idea for where you could order all of the dairy you need for the doughnuts."

If she thought I wouldn't notice that she wasn't answering my question, she was wrong. "Seriously, how long are you going to be?"

"I bought this amazing cheese from a local farm," she went on, ignoring me. "I mean, truly amazing. The guy makes milk, butter, and cream too. You guys should really think about ordering from him. Great products, no delivery costs. Local. Stinky Cheese Farm, it's called."

"Oh, yeah. I know about this place. The farmer's name is Riley, right?" Josh said.

"You know him?"

"I just know who he is. He grew up here, but he was away for college and stuff."

"I tasted the cream. It's out of this world. Like from magic cows or something."

"Magic cows?" I said.

"You know what I mean."

"We should check it out, right?" Josh said.

"Sure," I said.

"Great. I'll arrange it for you as a thanks for taking care of Zoe for an hour," Mom said and then ran up the stairs.

"An hour? Now it's an hour?" I yelled after her. "Sorry," I said to Josh. "You can go upstairs. I'll come up when she comes back."

"I'm fine here. Don't worry about it."

"Yeah," Zoe said. "We're fine here."

"So, what kind of food do you serve at Zoe's Purple Giraffe?" Josh said.

Josh was a natural at this stuff, way better than even Jeanine, who's been a big sister almost her whole life. Jeanine doesn't really do make-believe.

Zoe handed Josh a torn piece of construction paper with crayon scribbles in different colors. "Here's the menu."

Josh pretended to study it. "I'll have a hamburger and fries."

"Can't you read? We have spaghetti and carrot cake and cheddar bunnies," she read, following a scribble with her finger. "Where do you see hamburger and fries?"

"Sorry. I'll have the spaghetti then."

"Aw, too bad," she said as she flipped an ice cube into the air with a spatula. "We're all out."

This is where I'd have told Zoe I was finding another place to eat, but Josh just laughed and kept playing along.

After an hour and a half, Mom came back, and Josh and I finally headed up to my room to start figuring out the script for our supplier calls.

"I'm so sorry," I said as we climbed the stairs. "My friend Charlie never wanted to come over because we always ended up having to watch Zoe."

"Does he have any younger brothers or sisters?"

"A younger brother."

"So he probably does enough babysitting. It's just me at home, so I don't mind. Plus, Zoe makes me laugh. Are all little kids that funny?"

"You mean completely wacko?"

"I guess."

"I don't know, but I don't think so."

As I held the ladder still for Josh to climb up, I thought about why I hadn't told him that actually Charlie never does babysit for Justin. His parents used to ask him to, but he always said no, and they never made him. It felt bad, letting Josh believe something I knew wasn't true. I guess I just didn't want him thinking that Charlie was the kind of kid who wouldn't take care of his younger brother, even though he was.

Since it's hard to concentrate when your teeth are chattering, Josh and I worked in jackets, hats, and gloves. Judging from the ice crystals I found every morning in the glass of water I keep next to my bed, the Purple Demon had been keeping the attic at a toasty thirty degrees.

Though warmer, working in the living room was not an option.

Now that the family computer was set up in there, Jeanine was permanently camped out on the couch Skyping with Kevin Metz. She'd convinced him to email her photos of all the G&T assignments, and they reviewed the answers together on Skype. When they ran out of schoolwork, they'd play chess, study for the Solve-a-Thon, and giggle, at least Jeanine would. Kevin didn't say much except, "Nice move, Jeanine," or, "Sorry, Jeanine," every now and then. They'd even had a Skype sleepover.

It was a round-the-clock Skype-a-Thon, and I couldn't take it. Not because I felt stupid hearing them talk all that math, which was so beyond what I'd probably ever be able to do, it sounded like a different language. I hated that, but I was used to it. That wasn't the reason I walked around the house with earphones on. That was because Jeanine and Kevin were still JeanineandKevin.

I hadn't spoken to Charlie since he'd called about Thanksgiving, and I'd never emailed him back after he'd told me he'd made the basketball team. I tried to blame whatever was going on with us on my moving to Petersville, but every time I did, JeanineandKevin went off like an alarm. If they were still JeanineandKevin, why weren't we still TrisandCharlie?

By lunch, Josh and I were ready to make the calls. We downed grilled cheese sandwiches and then shut ourselves up in my parents' office.

I was so nervous dialing the first number, I could feel my heart beating in my fingertips.

"Lucky's Food Corp. May I help you?" said the lady who answered.

"Uh…" My mind had gone blank.

Josh held up our script.

"Excuse me?" the woman said.

I took a deep breath. "My name is Tris Levin, and I want to know how much it would cost to order some ingredients to make doughnuts."

"Uh-huh. And where is it you're calling from?" Something, gum probably, snapped painfully in my ear.

"Petersville."

"No, I meant, what company?" she said in a tone that made clear she thought I should have known what she'd meant.

"Oh, I'm not calling from a company. I'm calling from a stand, or it's not a stand yet, but it will be." This wasn't going at all how we'd planned. "I can't do this," I whispered and shoved the phone at Josh.

"No." He pushed the phone back at me. "Keep going."

"A stand?" the woman repeated. Another *pop*.

"Yeah, you know, like a lemonade stand? A hot dog stand? This is a going to be a doughnut stand, a chocolate cream doughnut stand." Now that I was saying the words out loud to someone other than Josh, I couldn't believe how stupid they sounded: I'm going to open a chocolate cream doughnut stand?

"I see, a chocolate cream doughnut stand. Really?" the woman said. She obviously couldn't believe how stupid the whole thing sounded either. I couldn't tell for sure, but I think maybe she was laughing a little too. "Then you need to speak to Sal. Hold on a sec. I'll connect you."

"Great, thanks," I said, but she was already gone. Maybe I was wrong, and she hadn't been laughing at me.

"What's happening?" Josh whispered.

"She's going to get Sal."

"Who's Sal?"

I shrugged. "The guy who deals with stands?"

Josh gave me a thumbs-up.

I don't know what this lady told Sal, but a minute later, a man had picked up and he was yelling, "Who is this?"

"Um, it's...this is—"

"Anton?"

"Who? No."

"How many times have we talked about this?"

"But this is—"

"You just keep quiet before you dig yourself in even deeper."

I must have looked like I felt because Josh whispered, "What's wrong? What's he saying?"

I shook my head and tried to get a word in with Sal.

"*Enough!*" Sal yelled so loudly that I almost dropped the phone. "You're gonna hang up this phone and go tell your mother you've been pranking again, and I mean now. Got it?"

"Got it," I said.

"What was that?" Sal said.

"Got it, sir," I said louder. Sal seemed like a sir kind of guy.

"All right then. See you tonight. But we're not done with this. Not by a long shot. Copy me?"

"Thank you." I was so relieved my time with Sal was coming to an end.

"Thank you? You still think this is funny?"

"No, sir. Sorry."

"Okay then."

"Bye," I said and hung up.

"Look at the bright side," Josh said when I told him what had happened. "You're not actually Anton. That kid won't know what hit him when Sal gets home."

14

Once I'd gotten my lines down, our food supplier calls went much better. And by better, I mean by the end of the day we'd gotten prices from everyone on the list, though one guy did insist on talking to "my mommy" before we talked business.

Josh and I had set a timeline for ourselves. We had only two weeks to figure out where we were getting our ingredients, but Mom made us promise we wouldn't make any decisions until we'd gone to Stinky Cheese Farm. She was sure it was the perfect place for us to buy the butter, milk, and cream we'd need, and Josh and I agreed that if we could get a good enough deal, it would be cool that the doughnuts were made with dairy from cows right here in Petersville. It might even be a good hook. *Starting Your Own Business for Dummies* says it's good to have a hook for your product, something that makes it especially cool or different.

Mom knew we were in a hurry to figure out our suppliers so she arranged for us to visit Stinky Cheese Farm the Saturday after Josh and I had made the calls. The catch was, she wanted Jeanine to go too. To sweeten the deal, she promised to take Josh and me to the movies if we could get Jeanine to come. Basically, she just wanted Jeanine to leave the house, which she hadn't done in days.

I hadn't seen a movie in forever. Back in the city, there was a theater three blocks away, but the closest one now was almost an hour's drive. I didn't even care what we saw. I just missed the whole sitting-in-a-dark-place-on-someone-else's-adventure feeling.

And the movie theater popcorn. I missed that too. What is it about movie theater popcorn?

When I came downstairs that morning, Jeanine was in her usual place on the couch studying for the Solve-a-Thon. Mom was there too, already working on her. "Not just cows, *baby cows.* Look how cute." Mom was shoving her phone right up in Jeanine's face.

"They're called calves," Jeanine said, underlining something in her study guide.

"You're not even looking."

"Because I don't care." Jeanine fled to the other side of the couch.

"C'mon," I said, "Josh is gonna be here any minute. You're not even dressed."

"I'm not going."

"We won't even be gone that long. We'll just bike there, see some cows, eat some butter, taste some cream. Then we're outta there, and you can come right back here and study for the rest of your life."

"I'm not interested, thanks."

If I weren't such a nuddy, I'd have gotten Mom to say she'd take us to the movies just for *trying* to get Jeanine to come with us.

Mom shuffled down the couch and shoved her phone in Jeanine's face again. "You haven't even looked. Tell me you don't want to see this adorable calf, and I'll leave you alone."

"I don't want to see this adorable calf."

"Well, I don't believe you."

"What happened to, 'I'll leave you alone'?"

"Ask Zoe how cute they were. Zo Zo, tell Jeanine how cute the baby cows were," Mom shouted.

"So cute!" Zoe called from the kitchen.

"See," Mom said.

"Are you saying they won't be cute after the Solve-a-Thon?" Jeanine said.

"Less cute."

"They're going to get less cute in two weeks? How much less cute exactly?"

"I wanna go see the cows again!"

"No! The cows need a Zoe break!" Mom yelled back.

"Why do the cows need a Zoe break?" I asked.

Mom didn't answer. Instead, she put her hand under Jeanine's chin and tipped back her head so she had to look up. "Please, honey, you need to get out of the house. It will actually make you study better. It's true. There's research."

"Where? Show it to me."

Mom didn't have any research. She had photos of cows, and those weren't getting the job done. There was no way we were getting Jeanine to Stinky Cheese Farm or anywhere else. Maybe we could get Josh's mom to take us to a movie if we let her pick which one. Really, I would have agreed to see almost anything.

"Jeanine, this is ridiculous." I could tell Mom was about to lose it because she was cracking her knuckles, something she tells us not to do. "Nobody needs to study this much. Plus, you'll love the farm."

"I can love it in two weeks," Jeanine said.

"Tom!" Mom yelled.

Dad appeared at the door to the living room. "What do you think?" He held up a picture frame filled with wine bottle corks all glued together.

"What is it?" I said.

"I made a corkboard. Get it? *Cork*board. For the restaurant, you know, for posting specials. What do you think?"

"Great idea, sweetie," Mom said.

Dad turned the frame around and admired it. "Yeah, I thought so too. And since we talked—"

"Tom, honey, I need you to focus."

"On what?"

"Jeanine doesn't want to go to the farm."

"What farm?" He was still smiling at his creation like he'd just invented tinfoil.

"Stinky Cheese Farm, remember? Tris and Josh are riding out there to talk to the owner, and it's so close, I thought Jeanine should go too. You know, to get out a bit." Mom had that just-say-what-I-say tone.

"Sounds good to me." No way did he actually remember.

"After the Solve-a-Thon," Jeanine said.

"After the Solve-a-Thon?" Dad said to Mom.

"That's not for two weeks," Mom said to Dad.

"That's for two weeks," Dad said to Jeanine.

"Tell her to go," Mom said to Dad.

"Go," Dad said to Jeanine.

"You can't make me bike someplace. It's physically impossible."

"This is true," Dad said. "But I could drive you and your bike over there, push both of you out, and then drive off."

"You're not funny," Jeanine said.

"Who's joking?"

"Honey, you need light and air. You're wilting," Mom said, petting Jeanine.

"I'm not a plant. I don't rely on photosynthesis for survival."

Mom cracked a few knuckles. "You know what I mean."

Jeanine laid the study guide down and looked at Mom. "What if I eat lunch on the porch?"

Mom twisted a finger, but it was all cracked out. "Fine. But you have to stay out for thirty minutes. And I'm locking the doors, I swear I am."

"Tell Riley I loved the Farmers' Wish!" Mom called from the porch as Josh and I walked our bikes down Terror Mountain.

"Farmers' Wish?" Josh said.

"Some cheese she bought when she was there. Those grilled cheese sandwiches she made, that's what she put in them."

"Oh, those were awesome!" Josh blew at the wall of hair hanging in front of his face. He needed both hands to keep his bike from taking off down the driveway. "But I think that bread your mom makes is awesome even on its own."

"I know. I don't think I can go back to store-bought now."

"Yeah, the packaged stuff is so much worse. It should be called something different."

"Like what?"

"I don't know." He thought for a minute. "Something like bread, but something less than bread, like maybe just…'ed.'"

"That's so good," I said, laughing. "The ads would be like, 'Why eat bread when you can have Ed? Ed never goes bad because it starts out that way.'"

"I was telling my mom the other day how good the homemade stuff is. She thinks it's really cool you guys make your own bread."

Josh had been spending so much time with us, it made sense he'd talked to his mom about what it was like at our house. I just hadn't thought about it before now. He'd probably told her that Zoe liked to eat frozen peas and uncooked pasta and that the Purple Demon got her kicks by turning out all the lights and that Jeanine studied for the Solve-a-Thon 24/7. I would have told her that stuff too if I were him. But it felt good to know he hadn't just told her about the crazy stuff.

"You know, making bread's not as hard as you think," I said. "I've done it with my mom. I could show you, I mean, if you wanted."

“Oh, yeah, definitely! And you think I could make it myself then?”

“Sure. I mean, you’d need a recipe, but yeah.”

“Cool! Maybe then I could surprise my mom with it, like for Christmas or something.” Even through all that hair, I could see he had a huge smile on his face.

I’d been trying not to think about Charlie since I’d gotten that last email. But right then, something popped into my head so fast, I didn’t have time to push it back out.

Charlie and I had never baked anything together.

He’d tasted almost everything I’d ever made. My peanut butter–white chocolate chip cookies were his favorite dessert in the whole world, or at least that’s what he said, but I’d never showed him how to make them himself, and he’d never asked me to. And somehow, I’d never thought how weird that was until right then.

At the bottom of Terror Mountain, we got on our bikes and pedaled off. The road was much flatter going away from town, and there were fewer patches of woods and more fields on either side.

“What do they grow here?” I asked as we passed a brown field covered in stubby stalks.

“Corn. It’s gone by the end of October, but in August, there’s a stand out here where you can buy it just picked.”

My mouth watered. Corn on the cob. Corn pudding. Corn muffins with whole kernels baked into them. Maybe even corn ice cream. I had to remember to tell Mom about the stand.

"Someone stands out here selling corn all day?" I asked.

"It's an honor stand."

"What's that?"

"You know, you're on your honor to pay. There's a sign with the price and a pile of corn and a box for the money, and you just put your money in the box and take what you pay for."

"Yeah, right."

"You've never heard of an honor stand?"

"Uh, no. Because that's crazy. Is there like a security camera or something?"

Josh laughed.

"And nobody steals the corn or the money or both?"

"I don't think so. I mean, they'd stop doing it if that happened."

"I bet if you did that in New York City, you know, put out a table on the sidewalk with a sign and a pile of corn and a money box, people would think it was some kind of trick. Like the corn was poisoned or something. Nobody would believe it was for real."

"That's kind of sad."

I didn't say anything. I didn't want Josh thinking living in the city was sad, even just "kind of sad." "Well, there *was* this flower shop on our block, and whenever Zoe passed by, the lady gave her some flowers for free."

"I think Winnie would run through town naked before she'd give anything away for free," Josh said.

I laughed. "Oh, and one time, this guy found my mom's wallet on the subway, and he tracked her down by calling the number on her bank card. So, I mean, it's not like nobody in the city has honor, you just don't *expect* them to, you know?" I pointed to a tangle of wood boards in a field on the right. "That must be it." Mom had told us that the road we needed to take was just past a collapsed barn.

"And there's the road," Josh said, pointing to a sign marking a dirt road.

"Hey, what do you know about this guy anyway?" I asked as we followed Valley View Road into a creepy forest of trees with white bark.

"Riley? Not much. My grandparents are good friends with his parents. They're not here anymore though. They moved to Florida when Riley took over. My grandfather says this place has been a dairy farm for, like, four generations. But it was always just milk till Riley took over."

We stopped when we saw the sign for the farm. STINKY CHEESE

FARM dribbled down it in red letters, and next to the words was painted a triangular block with lines all around it like Zoe puts around her suns.

"Is that supposed to be stink?" I said.

"Coming off the cheese? I think so."

I peered down Stinky Cheese Farm Road. A short ways ahead, the forest ended and fields began. "C'mon. Let's go."

On the other side of the woods, the land was open and flat all the way to the mountains. Fences lined both sides of the road, and behind them were white cows with black splotches and wiggling ears. There were big ones and little ones, and the big ones had bulging pink balloons that hung down between their back legs.

Up ahead, the road circled around the field on the right to a barn and a small house. Both were gray, but they must have been white at some point because there were places where bits of paint still clung on. Everything—fences, house, and barn—drooped as if too worn out to stand up straight.

The road here was rocky, and weeds had completely taken over in places, so we got off our bikes and walked them.

"Something stinks, but not like cheese," I said.

"I bet it's worse in summer."

"So what we're smelling is..."

"Cow poop."

"Great," I said and tried to breathe only through my mouth.

On the other side of the fence, a calf with black patches around each eye bounced through the grass next to me. "The baby ones *are* kinda cute."

Josh stopped. "Hey—is that him?"

Across the field, just in front of the barn, a guy in a black baseball cap was waving.

"Probably." I waved back.

The guy put his hands up, palms out like he wanted us to stop, so we did.

"You think we're going the wrong way?" I asked.

We watched as the guy then jogged over to a mud-splattered truck and got in.

"I guess he's coming to get us," Josh said.

"Makes sense. We *are* the customers."

"He looks pretty young to be running the whole place, huh?" Josh said.

"Yeah, in my head, farmers are old, but I think that's just because of the song."

"The song?"

"You know, 'Old MacDonald.' Zoe used to make my mom sing it over and over."

Josh and I watched the truck make its way toward us. I guess because the road was barely still road, he had to drive really slowly.

Finally, the truck pulled to a stop beside us. "Tris? Josh?" the driver said through the open window.

We both nodded.

"Cool. I'm Riley." He grinned and tipped his baseball cap. The stinky cheese symbol from the sign was printed on it in neon yellow. Up close, Riley looked even less like Old MacDonald. What he looked like was the guy who taught me keyboards at Ricky's School of Rock, right down to his thick black glasses, hoodie, and ponytail.

"I set up this whole tasting for you guys at the house. Jump in. We can throw those bikes in back," he said. Then he got out and helped us load the bikes.

Since the truck had just one row of seats, we both sat up front right next to Riley.

"So you guys are into doughnuts, huh? I think that's what that lady said."

"You mean my mom?" I said.

"With the little girl."

"My sister."

"She was *way* into the cows, which was cool, but you can't ride them," Riley said, all serious like we might actually not already know this.

"She tried to ride them?" Josh asked, trying not to laugh.

"I kept telling her: no riding the cows. But she wouldn't listen. I gave her some grain, you know. I said, 'Here look, you can feed 'em, and they eat right out of your hand.' But every time I turned around, she was trying to climb on."

Now I knew what Mom had meant about the cows needing a Zoe break.

Just then, we hit a bump, and Josh went flying into Riley. "Sorry," he said. Even with Riley driving super slowly, we were getting tossed all over the place. At least I could hold on to the door, but Josh was stuck in the middle with nothing to grab onto.

"No worries," Riley said. "So, tell me about these doughnuts."

"Well, we haven't actually made any yet. It's a long story," I said. Riley didn't need to know that this whole doughnut business had started with Mom and Dad making me do a project. That was just unprofessional. We were customers, and we were there to sample his products, and hopefully, make a deal. That was the only story Riley needed to know.

"You don't have to explain it to me, man. I get it. It's the dream, right? You just got to go for it. It can take a while to get there though, so don't lose hope. You just keep at it."

"Thanks. But I meant—"

"Like with me, all my life, my pops was like, this farm is going to be yours someday. And I was all like, 'No. Thank. You.' Getting up early is not for me. See, I was hard into the electronic music scene. I'd saved up and bought all my own gear. I had this sweet synthesizer. But all that equipment is super expensive. You need a computer and..."

What kind of business was Riley running? We didn't need to hear his whole story any more than he needed to hear ours. Why wasn't he talking about his products? Didn't he know the ABCs of selling? Always be closing the deal. That's the very first Selling Tip in *Starting Your Own Business for Dummies*.

"So I needed cash, and that's how I ended up working at this fancy French restaurant in Boston. And they had a cheese guy. One guy, his whole job was just cheese. He'd buy all these cheeses, put them out on this cart, and when people finished their meal, he'd like wheel it out so they could pick their cheeses. And I was like, 'Whaaaat?' because all I knew was cheddar and swiss and American. Maybe I'd had some provolone. But that was it. You know there's thousands of different cheeses?"

Here was my chance to focus Riley. "Actually—"

"Crazy, right? And each cheese has like its own story, where it's from, how it's made. Anyway, this guy—his name was actually Guy. Funny, right? But they don't say Guy. They say Geeeeey. It's French, whatever, anyway. So one day, Guy gave me this crazy, super melty, super stinky cheese, and it was like magic. I mean, one bite and I was hooked. I couldn't believe a food tasted like that. It was so different and so awesome. After that, Guy started teaching me all about cheese..."

Riley pulled up in front of the house but didn't stop talking. As we climbed out of the truck, Josh whispered, "It must be *really* hard to live out here all alone with nobody to talk to."

Something about Riley made me think he'd be like this even if he didn't spend all his time alone.

"So one time, Guy takes me with him to this farm in Vermont to a cheese tasting, and I was like *this* is it. *This* is what I'm gonna do! Like for life. I'm going to make cheese on my family's farm. And I told my dad, and he was so psyched that I wanted to come back and like do my thing here. He'd had it with those big dairy folks anyway, so he was like Riley, you do it your way. Your mom and I are hitting the beach. So I went back to school, changed my major from electronic music to agriculture, and now I'm here, living the dream. My girlfriend graduates in June, then she's moving up here. Maybe some friends too. It's a crazy lot of work."

We'd followed Riley onto the porch of the little house, and he pushed open the front door. "Hey, boys!" he called into a small room lined with shelves and hooks.

The second we stepped inside, two huge gray blurs—the "boys"

I guessed—were coming at us. Before I knew it, one of them had me pinned against the wall, his paws on my shoulders.

"Meet Ziggy," said Riley. "This one's Gonzo," he said of the other dog whose paws were on his own shoulders. Riley seemed to think this was a fine way to say hello. This was so not professional. I didn't need *Starting Your Own Business for Dummies* to know that.

"Hello, Ziggy," I said, looking up. Stretched out like that, Ziggy was taller than I was. Drool yo-yoed down at me from both sides of Ziggy's furry chin. I tried to turn my head to the wall to get out of range of the drool, but Ziggy dipped and blocked, and then all I could see was tongue.

"Uch!" I gagged.

Ziggy had licked my face so hard, he'd gotten saliva up my nose—his saliva. It hurt and it stunk. Ziggy's breath was toxic, and now it was inside my nose so I couldn't even get away from it.

"Wow! He really likes you," Riley said.

Gonzo dropped off Riley and mashed his head into Josh's side.

"Hey, Gonzo." Josh scratched the dog's back.

"Ziggy's kinda heavy." On top of the smell, I felt like my shoulders were about to separate from the rest of my body.

"Yup. Two hundred pounds of love, isn't that right, Ziggy?" Riley stroked Ziggy's head, and finally, Ziggy jumped down.

As Josh pet Gonzo, the dog flopped over, knocking Josh backward, and he had to grab onto a hanging raincoat to keep from falling.

"They love attention. Isn't that right, Gonzo?" Riley squatted and scratched the dog's belly. "What's this—oh no!" Riley rubbed something greasy off Gonzo's nose. "What did you do?" Riley suddenly sounded a whole lot like my mother. He stood up, marched down the hall, and disappeared into the room at the other end.

Gonzo popped up onto all fours.

"Gon*zo*! Zig*gy*!"

Ziggy whimpered. Then he and Gonzo slunk slowly off down the hall.

Riley appeared in the doorway. "Didn't I leave this door closed? Didn't I?" Now he really sounded like my mother.

The dogs stopped at the doorway and dropped to their bellies.

"Am I going to have to get a lock on the kitchen door?" Riley waited. Not surprisingly, the dogs weren't answering.

Josh looked at me.

"We can come back," I said.

"Don't look at me like you don't know what you did."

"He's still talking to the dogs, right?" Josh whispered.

One of the dogs, Ziggy, I think, barked.

"Yes, you do. And I'm very disappointed in you," Riley said, shaking his head.

The other one barked.

"You just stay there and think about what you did." Riley turned around. "Look at this mess."

"*Now* he's talking to us. C'mon," I said.

In the kitchen, broken glass covered the floor, and two chairs, snapped in half, lay in a pool of milk. "I don't know how that dog whisperer guy never loses his patience. I'm really sorry," Riley said.

"Oh, it's okay. Don't worry about it," Josh said because he's Josh. I didn't say anything.

"I had this whole tasting set up with crackers for the butter, and I made this awesome drink with the milk and some maple syrup."

"We can come back some other time," Josh said.

"Or maybe we could just do it at my place," I said, giving Josh a look.

Riley snapped his fingers. "Hey, I got it. Care package. Hold on. Two secs."

It took way more than two seconds, but eventually, Riley had put together the care package and Josh was bungee cording it to his bike rack.

"So you've got the butter, a pint of milk, and one of cream. And I put in some Farmers' Wish for your mom, and also something

I'm experimenting with, triple cream made of raw milk, super gooey, crazy stinky. It's wrapped in Riverbirch bark so you just scoop it out."

"Okay, thanks. We'll taste everything today and get back to you," I said.

"Yeah, stop by anytime. I'm always here."

"We'll email!" I called as we biked off. I didn't plan on visiting Stinky Cheese Farm again anytime soon.

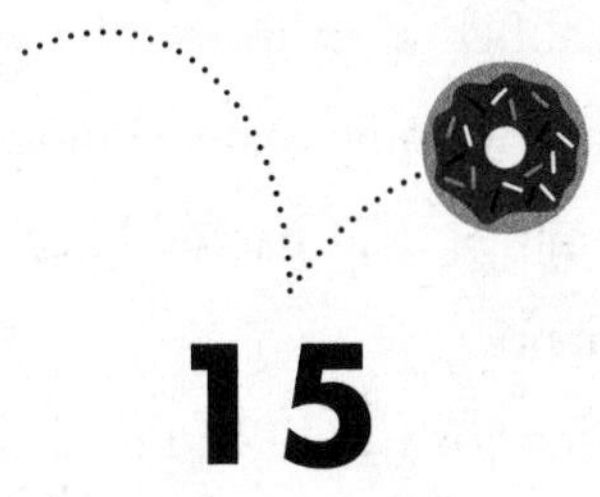

15

Mom was right. The Stinky Cheese Farm's butter, milk, and cream were all mind-blowing, and a great deal too because Riley wasn't going to charge for delivery since he was in Petersville anyway. His butter would be a little harder to work with because it came in different size lumps instead of sticks, but it was worth it. He weighed each so you knew how much you were paying for, but there was nothing on the package to help you measure out pieces like the lines printed on the paper around sticks of butter. I'd just have to use Mom's cooking scale to measure out what I needed.

We still had to make deals with suppliers for the other ingredients. To do that, the book said we were supposed to call back the wholesalers with the lowest prices and play them off each other to see if we could get them to go even lower. Since Josh and I didn't have the first clue how to do this, I decided to ask my dad for help. He'd done a lot of negotiating when he worked at the bank, so I thought he was qualified even though he was family. Besides, I had a feeling Winnie's warning against doing business with family applied more to siblings than parents. Just to be safe though, I decided not to tell her.

It was the day after Josh and I had made the calls. Dad was in his office reading another book about windmills. His latest plan was to put windmills up all over our property to harness the wind that constantly whips around our house, threatening to knock it down. He was sure that with the right number, we could power our whole house. He was super excited about it. He kept talking about how we needed to go to Denmark to see their windfarms, because they get something like half their electricity from wind there. I was terrified that this was the one project he'd actually stick with. He'd shown me photos of the windmills he wanted, and they were like something out of a sci-fi nightmare. It was bad enough up there on Terror Mountain without things that looked like Transformers towering over us.

"Dad, can I ask you something?" I said from the door to the office. "It's about the doughnut stand. It's kind of a business question."

He closed the book. "Sure. Fire away."

I went inside and showed him all the information Josh and I had gotten from the suppliers.

"So now we're supposed to negotiate for the best prices," I explained, "but something doesn't seem right about that. Isn't a price a price? I mean, you have the choice whether to buy something or not, but can you actually tell the seller to lower his price? Is that even legal?"

Dad laughed. "Yes, it's legal."

"Even if it is. It still feels weird, like something I shouldn't do."

"You got to get over that. You know what you need?"

"What?"

"A pitch, what you're going to say to convince these guys to lower their prices."

"Oh, yeah, they talk about that in the book."

"Yeah, a really good pitch," he said and stood up from his desk all of a sudden like he'd just remembered he had somewhere to be but then didn't go anywhere. "All right, take me through everything. This is going to be so great!"

I must have just been sitting there staring at him because then he clapped and said, "Come on! Get me up to speed. We've got a lot of work to do."

That's when I knew Winnie's warning about family did apply to parents, but by then it was too late.

"Okay, so first I made a list of—"

"Wait!" He grabbed my arm. "You know what we need?"

"No, what?"

"Supplies!" He sounded way too excited.

"I've got the book and paper and stuff."

"No. We need to be able to see all the information someplace. Visual representation of information is key. We'll need poster board and different colored Post-its and flags and markers and maybe a microphone so we can tape you and you can hear yourself doing the pitch and—are you writing this down?"

The good news was, Dad had found a new project, one he actually knew something about. The bad news was, that project was me.

Four hours and one trip to the office supply store in Crellin later, my parents' office had been transformed into Tom Levin's Negotiation Boot Camp. Every piece of information I had about the doughnut business was now color coded on Post-its and stuck to the wall along with a poster board with my pitch in bullet points, the words I was supposed to "punch" highlighted in neon orange. Dad had this theory that you had to "punch" the most important words in each sentence.

"I think I'm ready now." My voice was hoarse from practicing the pitch.

"Almost," he said. "You still need to hit those punch words harder."

"Okay."

"It's definitely better, much better, but I'm beginning to think what you really need now is a dry run."

"I've already run through it twenty times!"

"No, I mean live, with a real person, so you have to think on your feet. You need to know there's nothing wrong with negotiating, that you're not going to get into trouble. Otherwise, you won't sound confident, and confidence is key, right? The worst that can happen is somebody says no."

"Fine," I moaned. "What do you want to do?"

"Get your coat."

This was going to be painful. I could just tell.

Fifteen minutes later, my father pulled up in front of Renny's on Main Street.

"You want me to negotiate at the Gas Mart?" I said.

"Yup."

"But the prices are printed on everything."

"So?"

"You can't negotiate in a place like that!" Now I was getting angry. The stuff he'd made me do in the office was embarrassing enough but at least that was in private.

"Of course you can. A price is just whatever the seller and the buyer agree to. That's what I'm trying to teach you."

"Fine!" I yelled. "But this is it. I do this, and then I get to make the calls. No more practicing."

"This is it. I promise," he said.

"Okay. Let's get this over with," I said and got out of the car. Dad was smiling his big, goofy smile like this was about the most fun he could have.

Once inside, Dad walked slowly up and down the aisles studying the shelves, and I followed along behind. On our fourth loop around the store, I noticed the pimply kid behind the register eyeing us like we were going to steal something.

"So what should we get?" I whispered.

"These." He pulled a pair of sunglasses off a rack. "They sell these at the CVS in Crellin for ten dollars." The sticker on the glasses read "$11.99."

I looked at the glasses and then at the kid behind the register. "I don't know if I can do this."

"Yes, you can. Just do it," he said and handed me the glasses.

I didn't move.

"Now! Go!" he said, shooing me away.

There was no way my father was going to let me chicken out of this. This wasn't like deciding I didn't actually want to jump off that cliff into the waterfall on vacation last year in Mexico. People don't *need* to be able to jump off cliffs into waterfalls. But being able to negotiate? That, as my father had been telling me all afternoon, was a "life skill," something I had to learn how to do or I'd spend the rest of my life getting ripped off.

I turned around, walked to the register, and put the glasses on the counter.

The kid tipped his baseball cap back to look at me. "That'll be twelve dollars and ninety-two cents."

"Seems kind of high," I mumbled.

"What?"

"Seems kind of high."

"There are cheaper ones in there, I think." He pointed at the rack. "You want to go check?"

This wasn't how it was supposed to go. The guy was trying to be helpful, and now I was going to give him a hard time. I stood there for a minute not sure what to do next. Then I turned around and started back to the rack, but there was my dad, standing right in front of it, pumping his fist in the air. I guess it was supposed to be some kind of, "Hang tough, son," thing, but it just made me feel even more like a wimp. And not because I was too chicken to negotiate but because I was too chicken to tell my dad how stupid this was.

I took a deep breath and turned back to the register. "I'm not trying to give you a hard time, really. I want these glasses. It's just they seem like a lot, you know, for what they are. I was thinking they're more like ten-dollar glasses. That's what they sell them for at the CVS in Crellin."

The kid pulled off his cap, smoothed back his hair, and then put it back on. "So go to Crellin then, I guess."

"But don't you want my business?"

The kid looked over my shoulder at my dad who had this look on his face like he'd just seen me make a basket from the middle of the court in the last second of the game.

"Is this a dare?" the kid said.

"No. I'm just trying to negotiate with you. If you lower the price, I'll buy them here instead of going to Crellin."

"Man, I can't negotiate with you. This isn't my store. Do you know what Renny would do to me if he found out I was selling his stuff for less than he said to?"

I looked back at my Dad, who tick-tocked his head as he thought about this. Then he nodded and mouthed, "Okay."

"Okay," I said to the kid. "Sorry. I'll put them back."

"So it *was* a dare?"

"Not really."

"I don't get it. This is weird."

"I know. You're right. It is. Sorry," I said and walked out.

"So?" Dad said as we drove home.

"So what?" I said. "That was so embarrassing."

"But you didn't get in trouble. You didn't get arrested, right?"

"Right," I admitted.

"And you learned something else too."

"Yeah, don't negotiate at the Gas Mart."

"No. Make sure that the person you're talking to has the authority to negotiate."

"Oh, right, that too," I said.

By the time we got home, it was too late to make the calls, so first thing the next morning Dad and I locked ourselves back up in the office, and I called Pinehurst Food Corp., which had tied with Elwin Farms for the lowest prices.

"Hello, may I speak to Carl, please?" I said. Carl was the guy I'd spoken to the first time, and Dad said I should ask to speak to him again because it was important to develop relationships in the business world. Also, I knew Carl was the owner of the company, so he'd have the power to negotiate.

"For you, Carl!" shouted the man who'd answered.

A second later, Carl was on the line. "Yeah."

"Hi, Carl. This is Tristan Levin from Petersville. Maybe you remember—"

"Yeah, yeah. I remember. You ready to put in your order?"

"I'm actually calling about the price you quoted us."

"Yeah, what about it?"

"I just wanted to make sure that it was the *best* you could do for us. You know, because we're a *small* business just starting out and any additional *savings* we could get would really help. Also, even though I know we're not ordering *large* quantities now, if the doughnut stand does as well as we expect it to, we'll definitely be *increasing* those numbers."

I'd done my pitch perfectly. I'd punched my words. Not a single "um" and only one "you know." Based on what Dad had said, I fully expected the next words out of Carl's mouth to be, "Well, sure, I'd love to help you out, and I do think I can do a little better. How about we cut that price by five percent?"

But that's not what happened.

"What?" Carl said.

I repeated my pitch word for word a little louder this time, wondering if maybe Carl's hearing was going.

Turns out, Carl hears just fine.

"Let me get this straight. *You* want *me* to take my profit and pass it on to you. Is that right? Is that what I'm hearing?" Carl shouted into the phone. I looked at Dad and tried to hand him the phone, but he shook his head and pushed it back at me.

"No...um, I mean, I guess. It's just that we could really use that money to buy other stuff."

Okay, looking back, that was a really stupid thing to say. I just hadn't been prepared for someone to get all bent out of shape by my just asking if they could give us a better price. Dad kept saying the worst thing they could do was say no, but this was way worse than no.

"And what about *me*? What about *my* business? Don't I got other stuff I need that money for? Don't I got two kids heading off to college next year? *Twins!* I don't even get a break because they start the same year."

"I'm so sorry. I really didn't mean to offend you. I just thought that since Elwin Farms quoted us the same price, you might want the chance to underbid them."

"That's extortion. That's what that is."

"What? No. That's not what I meant." I turned to my father and whispered, "What's extortion?"

Dad chuckled, and I put my hand over his mouth.

"No, no, no. I know exactly what you're doing," Carl said.

"Please. Can I just explain?"

"No. You wanna do business with that slime bucket over at Elwin, you go right ahead. The two of you deserve each other," he growled and then hung up.

"Thanks a lot," I said to my father.

"Yeah, well, some people don't like you to negotiate. They take it personally."

"And wasn't this a piece of information you should have shared with me before I made the call?"

"Nah. This was way more fun," he said, grinning. "Besides it's all part of the learning process. I knew getting you guys to do these projects was a great idea."

I'd never missed school so much.

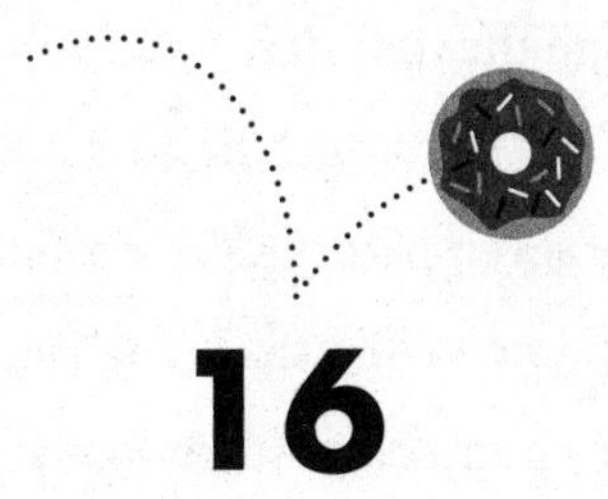

16

I don't know what Carl was talking about. Abe, the guy at Elwin Farms, wasn't a slime bucket at all. Though he didn't lower his prices, he did throw in free delivery because his delivery guy passed through Petersville anyway. He even said he thought the doughnut stand was a smart idea, and I'm pretty sure he meant it even though I was a customer, and *Starting Your Own Business for Dummies* says you should always say things to make your customers happy even if they're not true.

Once Josh and I had finalized the budget, I biked it over to Winnie, along with some molten chocolate cake to sweeten the deal. It took almost two hours and three molten chocolate cakes, but in the end, she settled for seven percent of the profit per doughnut. I knew Dad would have been impressed since I talked her down from twenty.

The book says you should always get everything in writing, so I told her I'd type something up on the computer at home and bring it back for her to sign the next day.

"Why wait? What if you get home and decide I don't even deserve the measly seven percent. Oh no, Slick. We're getting this down right here and now," she said. Then she pulled a typewriter out from under the counter and set it down in front of me.

"Oh, okay." I studied the machine. I'd never actually seen one up close. It looked way more complicated than a computer, which is kind of funny when you think about how much more computers can do.

Winnie slid a sheet of paper into the machine, then rolled it into place with what looked like a metal rolling pin. "All set."

Each time I hit a key, I watched one of the little metal arms swing up and smash its letter into the ink ribbon. After a couple of words, I accidentally punched an A instead of an S and asked Winnie how you delete.

"You don't," she said.

"But what happens if you make a mistake?"

"Don't."

"Too late," I said. "Didn't people make mistakes back when they used typewriters?"

"The newer models had correction keys, but this one is from

way back when people took enough time to be careful and just do things once."

"Well, I live in a time when we do things fast and sloppy and have to do them over and over again, so what am I supposed to do?"

"No need to get all snippy, Slick. Just *X* it out and start again, and this time don't make any mistakes."

Know what happens when someone tells you not to make mistakes?

That's right. It took me almost ten tries before I got it right, where right meant my own name had a typo.

"Congratulations," Winnie said. "Now we need another one."

"What?"

"Both parties need an original. Doesn't your book say that?"

Unfortunately, it did. "Can't you type the second one?"

"Oh, fine."

I turned the typewriter around and handed her the agreement.

"So let's see..." She squinted at the paper, then at the typewriter keys. "First word...agreement. *A...A...A...A...* There it is. *A*." She punched the key, then squinted back down at the paper. "Yup. *A*. Okay, what's next? *G...G...G...G...*"

She didn't make a single mistake, but she took even longer than I had.

When we finally had two agreements, and we'd each signed

both of them, Winnie pulled some cards from her pocket and handed them to me. "Don't screw it up or sell it to Martha Stewart."

"Is she that blond lady with the magazine?" I asked, flipping through the three chocolate-stained cards.

"All you need to know is she'd kill to get her hands on that recipe, and she's already done hard time so I wouldn't put it past her. Point is, you keep it to yourself. Got it?"

"Got it," I said.

Then I ran across the street to show Josh, and we celebrated by eating more molten chocolate cake and figuring out how many doughnuts we'd have to sell to become millionaires.

Biking home, I could feel Winnie's recipe in my pocket every time my right leg came up, and when it did, the smile I'd been wearing since I'd left the General Store got even bigger. The sides of my face hurt, but the smile had taken over, and I couldn't shut it down, no matter how hard I tried. My whole body was smiling.

Suddenly, Charlie popped into my head, but this time I didn't push him right back out again like I had been.

I had news...huge, smile-so-big-it-hurt news. I had to call Charlie now. I had to *want* to call him now. Didn't I?

I waited for my legs to pump faster because I couldn't wait to get home and call him.

I waited for my brain to start putting together the words I was going to use to tell him about everything I'd done to get those three cards in my pocket.

I waited to finally feel okay that he never was going to send me those sorrys I still looked for in my inbox.

But my legs didn't pump faster, and my brain didn't look for words, and I did not feel okay. My smile finally gave out, and I biked off the side of the road into a field of dead grass, tipped myself onto the ground, and looked up at the white sky.

I didn't want to talk to Charlie. I wanted to want to, but that wasn't the same.

I didn't want to hear him talk about basketball and how unfair it was that Coach Stiles wasn't giving him more playing time.

I didn't want to hear him repeat all that dumb stuff his dad always says, the stuff now he always says.

Most of all, I didn't want to hear him say how crazy it was to think a doughnut could change your life.

I did miss Charlie, but not the one who'd answer the phone if I called when I got home. I missed the Charlie who refused to go to yard the day I thought I'd killed Charlotte K. But that kid was gone. He'd slipped away so slowly, it had been easy to pretend he was still there. But he hadn't been, not for a long time, not since way before the move. And neither had TrisandCharlie.

I wanted to jump back on my bike and race home, leaving

everything I was feeling out there. But I couldn't move. My chest hurt like something was trying to crush it, and I just had to lie there and take it.

I don't know how long I lay there staring into the blank sky pinning me to the ground, but by the time it finally let me up, it had started going gray.

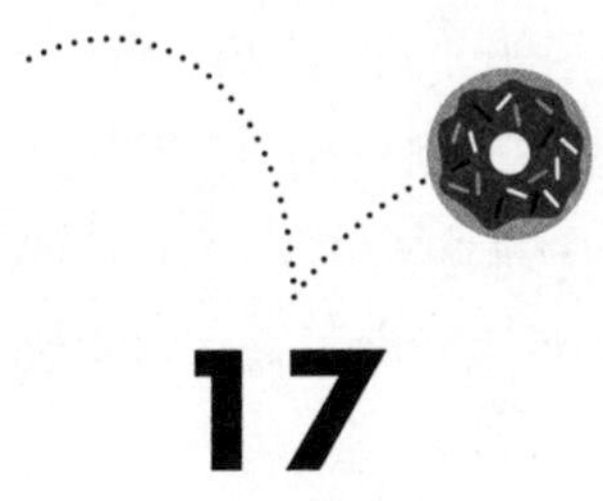

17

I'd planned Doughnut Day so I could have the kitchen all to myself. I didn't want anyone looking over my shoulder or telling me I was messing up. And I definitely didn't want anyone with me if it turned out these doughnuts weren't what I'd been dreaming they'd be all this time. Dad was taking Jeanine to the Solve-a-Thon. And Mom was going to keep Zoe busy playing Peter Pan in the basement, where, thanks to the zip line Jim the Kidnapper had installed, she could fly even without happy thoughts or fairy dust.

I didn't want to waste any time on Doughnut Day, so the night before, I got out the equipment I'd need, including the fancy pastry gun Mom had gotten me.

I'd been practicing using the gun, and if I pressed down the plunger really fast with the gun at just the right angle, I could shoot icing onto a cake from halfway across the kitchen. Not that you'd ever need to do that, but it got me thinking that the police should consider trading in their guns for ones that mow people down with a stream of cream or mousse or something like that because then, if they've got the wrong guy, big deal. It's kind of genius, right? Not in an I-can-solve-three-hundred-math-problems-in-six-hours kind of way, but still.

When my alarm went off at seven thirty the next day, I got dressed, grabbed the pastry gun—I'd decided it was too valuable to leave out in the kitchen all night—and climbed down the ladder.

I knew Jeanine would have gotten Dad up at the crack of dawn for the Solve-a-Thon, but I was worried Mom might still be in bed. She'd been staying up late trying different chicken pot pie recipes. She'd decided chicken pot pie was a must for the restaurant but that hers needed some kind of twist. The one she'd made with beets had bright pink puff pastry on top, which was definitely different, but none of us loved the taste, so she was still experimenting.

"Levin. Tris Levin, licensed to fill." I threw open my parents' bedroom door, pastry gun aimed at the bed.

"Mom?"

The bed was empty, and the mattress had been stripped.

I heard a moan and followed it to the bathroom. There, lying on the floor, curled around the toilet in her bathrobe, eyes closed, was my mother.

This was bad—bad for Doughnut Day, bad for me, and, thinking about it now, bad for Mom too, though I have to admit, I wasn't so focused on her at the time. At that moment, seeing her there on the floor, all I wanted to do was shout, "Get up! It's Doughnut Day! My day! I've earned this day. I deserve this day. So whatever you have, suck it up!" But I didn't. Instead, I said, "Are you okay?"

She moaned a "no" and hugged the toilet a little tighter.

"Did you throw up?"

Yes moan.

"More than once?"

She held up four fingers.

"Feel better?"

No moan, louder and longer than the first.

"You wanna try to get up?"

"Tile. Good. Cold," she said, eyes still shut.

"But..." I knew I shouldn't say it, but I couldn't stop myself. "It's Doughnut Day, remember?" I held up the pastry gun. "So you *are* getting up soon, right?"

She opened one eye and glared at me with it.

"Okay. Sorry. I was just asking because," I said to myself as I moped away, "how do you *know* you won't feel better playing Peter

Pan in the basement than you do lying on the bathroom floor unless you try?"

What's the worst that could have happened? She'd already thrown up four times. What was once more? Maybe that last fifth vomit was just what she needed?

I'd thought my father and Jeanine had left already, but when I got downstairs there they were, Dad sitting at the kitchen table drinking tea and Jeanine standing at the front door, jacket zipped, earmuffs secured, several razor-sharp number two pencils in each mitten.

"Dad! It's 8:03…8:03!" she shouted, pointing at the clock on the wall. "Remember what I said? No later than eight o'clock."

Dad sipped his tea. "Jeanine, you can't pretend you don't hear me just because you don't like what I'm saying."

"Oh yeah? What makes today different from all other days?" I said.

"I'm just thinking, maybe we shouldn't go because Mom's sick and you were going to make the doughnuts today."

"Really?" I said. Was Dad actually thinking about choosing my Doughnut Day over one of Jeanine's math competitions? Was it April Fools' or something?

"What are you saying?" Jeanine was still going with the "if I don't hear what you're saying, it's not happening" strategy.

"I know Tris could make the doughnuts another day, but he had this all planned. It seems a little unfair. Plus, it's just another Solve-a-Thon. Missing one isn't the end of the world."

"But it *is*! It *is* the end of the world!" Jeanine said, nodding like some creepy bobblehead.

"Honey, you've got to keep this stuff in perspective."

"Perspective? You want *me* to keep this in perspective? You want me to miss a *major* math competition so Tris can shoot cream into balls of fried dough?"

"Now that's not fair," Dad said. "He's put a tremendous amount of work into this project."

"What about the work *I've* put into studying for the Solve-a-Thon? I never get credit for doing work because I like to work. I work all the time, so it doesn't matter. You don't even care, but Tris wants to make a few doughnuts and you throw him a party!"

The craziest thing about what Jeanine was saying was that I could tell she actually believed it.

"We're not throwing him a party," Dad said, chuckling.

"Don't laugh at me!" Jeanine rushed at him with her number two pencils held out like daggers.

"Calm down. You know how proud we are of you. And we drive you all over the place for all kinds of things, the Solve-a-Thons, the spelling bees, the National Geography Bees—"

"The Math Olympics," I added.

"But you said I could go to *this* Solve-a-Thon."

"It's *one* Solve-a-Thon," Dad said. "What's the big deal?"

"You don't get it!"

"Come on, Jeannie." Dad tried to wrench the pencils away from her. "Take off your jacket. Sit down. Let's figure this out."

"No! I *need* this Solve-a-Thon. I *need* to be doing more math."

"So fine. Do more math. The internet's working. I can print out as many math problems as you want. You can spend a whole week doing math problems."

"It won't help!" She dropped her pencils and crumpled to the floor.

Dad crouched over her. "I still don't understand. How come?"

"Because there won't be other people. I won't be getting smarter."

"That doesn't make any sense."

"How will I know how good I am unless I can see how many people are worse than me?"

"Okay. Now you're scaring me."

"You don't understand!" She covered her face with her mittens and curled into a ball under the kitchen table.

I'd never seen her go quiet like that in the middle of a tantrum. Louder and whinier till her opponent can't take it anymore is her usual strategy.

"So explain it to me then," my father said. "What makes *this* Solve-a-Thon so important?"

Jeanine didn't say anything. I was pretty sure she was crying.

"Come on." Dad stuck his head under the table. "Explain it to me."

"Because I don't have anything here." Jeanine's voice was so small it didn't even sound like hers.

"Where?"

"Here. Petersville. I don't have Mathletes. I don't have G&T. I don't have Kevin. I don't even have normal school. I don't have anything, and...and Tris has everything!" she blurted out.

"What is she talking about?" I said to my father.

"You *know* what I'm talking about!"

I stuck my head under the table now too. "No, I don't."

She sat up and looked at me. "You like it here!"

"What?"

"You do! You like it here."

"I do not!" I said like she'd just accused me of picking my nose.

"Yes, you do. I've seen you!"

"Seen me what?"

"You like Josh, and you like that crazy lady at the General Store and hockey and your doughnut business. You even like biking around. You like it here!"

I opened my mouth to tell her she was wrong, but then something made me stop.

I couldn't believe it: she was right!

When had that happened? When had I stopped waking up in the wrong bed in the wrong room in the wrong town?

"And I know you don't talk to Charlie, so you don't even want to go back. You're not even friends with him anymore!"

It was the first time anyone had said it out loud, and it hurt more because I hadn't seen it coming.

"Jeanine!" Dad said.

I couldn't tell if my father wanted her to stop because what she was saying about Charlie was mean or because it was true or both.

"And I don't have one thing here. Not one friend or activity, not one anything."

"I know," I said. "Because you never leave the house. You won't try."

"That's not it. You know that wouldn't matter. You know it! I'm just not like you."

"Yeah, I know. You're smart."

"Come on, Tris. You're smart," Dad said.

"Not like her. It's okay. I'm not stupid or anything, but I'm not smart like her."

Dad didn't say anything.

Jeanine got on her knees so that she was facing me. She wasn't crying anymore, but she looked sadder than I'd ever seen her. "But you're good at this. You just made all this stuff happen here. I can't do that. I'm not good at Petersville."

I can't even tell you exactly what that meant, "good at Petersville," but she was right about that too. Whatever it meant, I was and she wasn't. And Petersville wasn't something like basketball she could choose not to do. She'd just have to get up and do it badly every day till one day she either got better or left. And maybe she would get better when she started school, but maybe she wouldn't. Maybe she'd wake up with that feeling that she was in the wrong bed in the wrong room in the wrong town every morning till she was old enough to go someplace right. My parents would have said that was impossible, that it would just take time, but that's what parents have to say. The truth is they have no idea.

"I'm sorry." I wasn't even sure what I was apologizing for, but I felt bad. Maybe Josh was rubbing off on me.

"It's okay. It's not your fault."

"But maybe I could help." I slid off my chair so I was kneeling under the table now too. "I mean, I know I was weird when you asked Josh to join your book club, but it's okay with me if you still want him to."

"Thanks." She gave a little smile, but she still looked so sad.

"And...maybe, maybe I could make the doughnuts while I take care of Zoe so you could still go to the Solve-a-Thon." I couldn't believe what I was offering.

"Really?" Jeanine said.

"Really?" Dad said.

"Yeah, sure. As long as Dad makes sure Zoe gets that I can't play all day." Even if it didn't work, I could always make the doughnuts the next day. The Regional Solve-a-Thon wouldn't roll around again for a year.

"Done." Dad reached out to shake my hand before I could change my mind. "Zoe!"

"*What?*" Zoe yelled from the living room.

"Come here!"

"*Why?*"

"*Now!*"

A moment later, Zoe appeared in the doorway in her ski jacket and fairy wings. "Don't yell. It hurts my concussion." She'd been in and out of concussions since my father's accident.

"What did we talk about yesterday? When I call, you come. Period."

"I don't remember yesterday. You know, concussion," she said, pointing to her head like my dad was a complete nuddy.

Dad rolled his eyes and said something in French that sounded like, "*Deeeuh meh deh!*"

"What did *I* do?" Zoe said.

"Nothing," Dad said.

"Then why are you Frenching at me?"

"Just listen. Mommy's sick and has to rest and I have to take Jeanine to the Solve-a-Thon, so Tris is going to play with you, but he's also going to be making his doughnuts, so you have to play quietly while he's working in the kitchen. Okay?"

"Okay," she said and skipped off.

"Okay?" he said to me.

"Okay." It so wasn't, but it was too late to back out now.

"All right, Jeanine, thank your brother. Let me just tell Mom. Hopefully, she's made it off the bathroom floor by now," he said as he climbed the stairs.

Jeanine and I crawled out from under the table and began collecting her pencils. "You really think you'll be able to make the doughnuts with Zoe around?" she said.

I shrugged.

"Hey, um, I'm sorry for before, you know, for what I said about Charlie."

"It's okay. It's true. But it's okay, I think. He and I weren't friends like...like you and Kevin are. I just didn't know it."

"Oh. I'm still sorry." She looked down at her pencils.

"We missed one." I pointed to a pencil that had rolled over by the stove, and Jeanine picked it up.

"I know you haven't known him that long or anything, but Josh is really nice. It's good you met him."

"Yeah, it is."

"All right, let's get this show on the road," Dad called. A second later, he was jogging down the stairs.

Jeanine pulled her hood up and Velcroed it under her chin. "Hey, if you can't get the doughnuts done, maybe I can help you make them tomorrow, okay?"

"Sure. Hey, good luck," I said.

"Thanks...also thanks for..." She trailed off.

"I know. You're welcome."

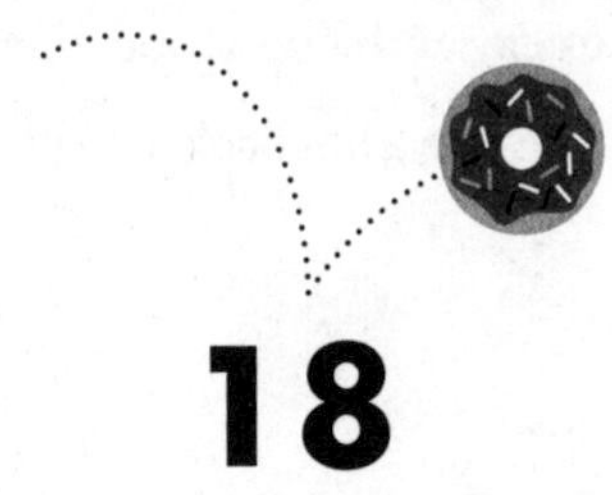

18

"But I told you we're taking turns!" I yelled at the bathroom door. Zoe had locked herself inside and was holding my pastry gun hostage.

"Dad said you had to play Peter Pan."

"Really? Is that what Dad said? Because what *I* remember him saying is that you have to let me bake."

"Oh, yeah! *I* remember that too," she said like she was all excited we had this in common.

"Okay, so come out, I'll bake, and *then* we can play Peter Pan."

"But Dad never said which came first, Peter Pan or doughnuts. Why can't Peter Pan go first?"

I thought for a minute. "Look, if you come out right now, and be good till I finish making the dough, I'll give you fairy dust to play Peter Pan with."

The door flew open, and Zoe stood there, a band of lotion painted under each eye like a linebacker. "What fairy dust?"

Thirty minutes later, I had my first blob of doughnut dough. I'd followed the recipe more carefully than I'd ever done anything in my life, but since I'd never made doughnuts before, I had no clue how I'd done.

The dough felt good, soft like new Play-Doh and cold and sticky too, but it didn't feel different from any other blob of dough I'd touched before, so who knew? I'd just have to wait and see, which made me nervous but also kind of excited. I covered it with plastic wrap, then put it in the pantry to rise. It would need two hours, which gave me plenty of time to play with Zoe and make the cream.

"You can come out now!" I called.

Zoe climbed out of the cardboard box she'd dragged into the kitchen and pulled the masking tape off her mouth. "Where's my dust?"

Just so you know, the cage and muzzle were Zoe's idea. I'd told her that if she touched or said anything while I was cooking, our deal was off, and she didn't want to take any chances.

"It's coming," I said. Then I went back into the pantry and put two handfuls of King Arthur All-Purpose Flour into a ziplock bag.

"That's it?" said Zoe, frowning when I handed her the baggie.

"That's it," I said.

She studied it, then ran a finger through the powder. "This is just flour!"

"Sure, if you use it to cook, but not if you use it for, uh, whatever fairies use fairy dust for."

"But it's not special."

"Think of it this way—fairies have wands, right?"

"Yeah."

"And what are wands made out of?"

"I don't know. Sticks?"

"Exactly. They're just sticks till fairies use them as wands. This is just flour till a fairy uses it as fairy dust. Same thing, right?"

"I guess." She was studying the flour again. "But there's so little."

"That's because this is the powerful stuff, the deluxe dust. A tiny pinch goes a long way. But maybe you can't handle it. Maybe I should get the rookie stuff." I took the bag away from her.

"What's rookie stuff?"

"It's for the new fairies who don't know what they're doing."

"It's not flour?"

"No way. The rookie stuff is cornstarch. Maybe that would be safer."

"Noooooo, deluxe dust! Deluxe dust!" she said. Then she snatched back the baggie and raced to the basement door.

Down in the basement, I helped Zoe put on and tighten her harness. Then we climbed to the landing halfway up the basement stairs, and I clipped her onto the zip line.

"First, I must throw the fairy dust on you," she sang. Then she took a pinch of flour and tossed it in her face.

"Ready?"

She sneezed and gave me a thumbs-up. I let go, and she squealed all the way down to the other end of the basement.

After five minutes of *clip in, walk down, clip out, walk back up, repeat,* I was bored out of my skull. That's when I decided to see if I could teach Zoe to clip in and out herself. I would never have left her there alone, but at least that way, I could use the time to go over step two of the recipe.

It took a couple of tries but eventually she figured out that if she used both hands, she could pull back the little lever on the clip and slip it over the zip line. Once it was on, there was no way she could get hurt since Jim the Kidnapper had gotten these extra safe clips used by mountain climbers. So for the next hour, Zoe clipped herself in and out of the zip line, I memorized how to make the chocolate cream, and everybody was happy. Zoe didn't even complain when I told her it was time to go back upstairs, mostly because she was out of fairy dust by then.

Zoe didn't want to stay in the kitchen for step two, so I told her she could play in her room till I was done.

Winnie had warned me that the chocolate cream was the hardest part of the recipe, but it turned out that it was just like making pudding. With pudding, you have this runny, melted chocolate mixture, and you're stirring so long you feel like your arm will fall off, but the chocolate never looks any thicker. Then, just when you can't stir one more second, something changes. The runny mixture becomes something new that wasn't there before, something somewhere between liquid and solid. The secret is just the belief that if you keep stirring, you will eventually get there before your arm falls off.

It was that way with the cream. I'd been stirring forever when suddenly the waves I made with my spoon were there even when the spoon was gone.

I dunked my finger and tasted.

Sweet. Creamy. Rich. But something was wrong.

I took another bite.

Good, definitely good, but *just* good. No more than good.

I hadn't done all this work just for good! People didn't write articles about good or dream about good or get up at the crack of dawn to eat good. Good was not life changing! My insides suddenly felt like they were on spin cycle.

Had I forgotten something? I grabbed the recipe. No. I'd done everything just like I was supposed to.

So what did this mean?

Were life-changing doughnuts like the Tooth Fairy or the Man in the Moon or every other bit of magic in this world? A complete lie?

Had the people of Petersville been deprived so long they couldn't tell the difference between a good doughnut and a life-changing one?

I put the cream in the fridge and sprinted upstairs.

"Mom?" I whispered. She'd made it to the bed and was pretty clearly asleep. "Mom?" I said again, louder this time.

"Mmm."

I lay down beside her and whispered right in her ear, "I made the cream."

"Mmm."

"It tastes like chocolate pudding."

"Mmm-hmm."

"Mom, please, wake up," I begged, squeezing her shoulder.

"I'm up. I'm up. What she'd do?"

"Nothing. But the chocolate cream tastes like chocolate pudding."

"What?"

"For the doughnuts. The chocolate cream tastes like chocolate pudding."

She pressed her hand to her stomach. "Can you not talk about food, please?"

"Mom, please! I need your help."

She sat up slowly. "Okay, okay. Let's just not say the words. So the...the C tastes like P. What's wrong with that?"

"It just tastes like normal pud—sorry, I mean, P. Not amazing P or C or whatever, and it has to be amazing."

"Ah, good not great. I'm familiar with the problem."

"Yeah, good not great." I knew she'd get it.

"Was it still hot, the C, when you tasted it?"

"Yeah, warm."

"Finish. Finish the recipe. Make the doughnuts, I mean, the D. Make the D, fill the D, then decide. The whole is always bigger than the parts when you're talking food. The magic happens when you put them together. PB&J is a totally different animal from the PB and the J and some B, right?"

"I guess. Okay, I'll finish and then see." I was still worried, but it's not as if I had a lot of options. "Sorry I woke you."

"Be careful when you fry, you know, because the oil—"

"I know."

"How's it going with Zoe?"

"Fine. She's in her room."

Or so I thought. But as I found out when I went to tell her that I was ready to go back down to the basement, Zoe was not in her room.

Or the living room.

Or the kitchen.

Or Jeanine's room.

Or any of the other places I checked in the hope that I was wrong about where I thought she'd gone.

Finally, I went back to the kitchen and threw open the basement door. A powdery cloud wafted out.

"Zoe?"

"Don't come down here!"

I started down the stairs. The cloud thickened.

"Zoe!"

White powder carpeted the basement like fake snow in the Christmas windows on Fifth Avenue. Four empty gallon bags of King Arthur Flour sat crumpled on the landing.

"Go make doughnuts!" Zoe appeared out of the flour mist like a zombie in a horror movie.

"Mom's gonna kill you."

"Na-unh. I'm gonna clean it up."

"How?"

"Dustbuster, nuddy," she said as she clipped in and zoomed off. But this time, instead of squealing, she coughed and was coughing so hard by the time she reached the end, she couldn't unclip herself.

"My eyes hurt," she said, rubbing them.

I helped her down. "Let's get out of here."

"But we have to clean up."

"*We?* You mean you and Tawatty Tawatty Dabu Dabu."

"They can't help." She plopped down on a mound of flour, and it whirled up around her. "They're gone."

"Where'd they go?"

She stared at the floor.

"Zoe, do you know where they went?"

"Home home." Her bottom lip quivered.

I guess Zoe was still waking up in the wrong place too.

"C'mon. Let's go," I said.

She didn't move.

"Don't you want to help fill the doughnuts?"

The corners of her mouth twitched. A second later, both arms shot in the air.

"Forget it," I said.

Her arms jerked higher.

"Ugh, fine," I groaned as I hoisted every last bowling ball of her onto my hip, and clawed my way up the stairs.

I poured water over her eyes in the bathroom until they felt better. Then we went into the kitchen and rolled out the dough together. Once it was half an inch thick like the recipe said, I let Zoe cut out circles with the top of a glass like Mom had taught us to do for biscuits.

Hot oil plus Zoe seemed like an even worse combination than chili peppers plus chocolate, so back in the box she went while I fried the doughnuts. It took only two minutes for the dough circles to puff up golden, but the whole process took a while because I could only fry two at a time, and as soon as I took them out of the oil, I had to roll them in a mixture of sugar, salt, and vanilla bean.

When all ten doughnuts were fried and sugared and cool enough not to burn off your fingerprints—I'm missing four—I put Zoe on a stool at the counter and handed her the gun filled with cream.

"Okay. Now, nice and slow," I said and carefully pushed the tip of the gun into a doughnut.

As Zoe squeezed the plunger, the doughnut inflated like it was taking a breath.

"Whoa!" she said, her eyes widening with the doughnut.

Before long, chocolate oozed out the other side.

"Okay, that's good… Stop… Stop! *Stop!*"

"You don't have to yell," she said, finally letting go.

"Watch it or I'll French at you."

Zoe rolled her eyes. "You can't French."

I held the doughnut up close to my face and breathed it in.

Cinnamon French toast…funnel cakes…hot chocolate… My mouth went off like a sprinkler. *Please, please, please let them taste as good as they smell,* I prayed. I crossed my fingers, opened my mouth, and—

Ow!

I looked down just in time to see Zoe pulling away. There was a wet mark on my sleeve.

"You bit me? I let you use the gun and you bit me?"

Zoe's bottom lip puffed out. "*I* wanna doughnut."

"And you'll get one."

"But how come you get to go first?"

"Because *I* made them."

"*I* helped."

I thought for a minute then held up the I-mean-business finger my parents are always using on Zoe. "Don't ever bite me again. You want to bite everybody else, that's up to you, but not me. Got it?"

"Got it. We don't bite Tris."

"All right then, here." I handed her the doughnut. "Don't eat yet. Just hold it."

Zoe cradled the doughnut as if it were a living thing.

I took another doughnut and shot it full of cream. "Okay, ready?"

She nodded.

"Three…two—"

"One!" Zoe yelled and crammed as much of the doughnut as would fit into her mouth.

I was still holding mine. It was weird, but after everything I'd done, suddenly I couldn't take a bite. If it *was* just a good doughnut, I didn't want to know.

"Mmm," Zoe moaned and gobbled up the other half. That was a pretty good sign, but it didn't mean much since I could fill a dog biscuit with chocolate cream and Zoe would go crazy for it. But then, with chocolate leaking out of the corners of her mouth, Zoe said, "I don't want to be president anymore. When I'm growed up, I'm gonna be a doughnut maker too!"

That's when I had to know: Had I really just made life-changing doughnuts?

I took a bite, then closed my eyes and focused on all the different things happening in my mouth: springy cake bursting with vanilla; sugar and salt crystals crunching between my teeth; waves of chocolate rolling slow and smooth across my tongue. Mom had been right. The whole was so much bigger than the parts, so much bigger even than something you just tasted. Taste was only in your mouth. This went zinging all over from my toes to my fingers to my brain.

Phew…these *weren't* just good doughnuts. They were picture-in-the-paper-get-up-at-dawn-flying-carpet doughnuts.

Phew? Yeah, it's not how *I* thought I'd feel either. Sure, I'd expected a little phew, but mostly what I'd expected was *Shazzam!* And there was none of that. Just phew and kind of a now-what emptiness.

What was wrong with me? Why wasn't I taking my victory lap around the kitchen? Or running for the phone to call Josh? Or running upstairs to tell Mom? Or just plain shoving another mind-blowing doughnut in my mouth?

"I don't feel so good," Zoe said and lay down on the kitchen floor.

I looked over at the tray of doughnuts. Two unfilled ones were missing.

Zoe lifted her shirt and looked down. "Belly says doughnuts are bad."

"Tell Belly not to be such a pig," I said and lay down on the floor next to her. The phew was gone, and all that was left was the now-what emptiness growing bigger every second like a black hole.

"Does your tummy hurt too?"

"Sort of."

"Make circles. It helps," she said, petting her belly.

"I don't think circles will work this time."

As Zoe groaned and rolled around on the floor next to me, I tried to happy thought my way to *Shazzam*:

Happy Thought #1: Winnie's doughnuts were mind-blowing.

Happy Thought #2: Winnie's doughnuts were going to make the Doughnut Stop a huge success.

Happy Thought #3: Winnie's—

And that's when it hit me. I knew what was wrong. And I knew exactly what I had to do to fix it.

I jumped up and ran around the kitchen gathering ingredients.

"What are you doing?" Zoe groaned.

"Making more doughnuts."

"Uggg. Why?"

Mom always talked about needing to make a recipe her own, but I'd never understood why before now.

Anybody could follow a recipe. Robots could do that and even did in those big cookie factories where they made Oreos and Fig Newtons. But those robots weren't really *making* something; they were just following instructions the same way they do when they make cars or anything else. I didn't want doughnuts from the Doughnut Stop to be something a robot could make you with Winnie's three cards. I wanted to put something of me in there too.

Robots couldn't change a recipe. They did everything exactly the same each time. But I didn't have to. I'd followed enough recipes to know how they worked, and I could experiment and make this recipe my own. I didn't mean I wanted to make Tris Levin's Chocolate Cream Doughnuts. That's not what this was about. The chicken soup Mom made was still Grandma Esme's Cold Cure Soup even though she never made it exactly the same way. Without Winnie, Petersville never would have had chocolate cream doughnuts, and without her recipe, I'd never be able to bring them back. They'd always be Winnie Hammond's Famous Chocolate Cream Doughnuts. I just hoped I'd be able to get her to understand that when I told her that I'd tinkered with her recipe. I was less worried about how Josh would take it since I was pretty sure he'd be okay with it as long as the doughnuts were still mind-blowing.

I ran to the refrigerator and pulled a bowl of leftovers from the top shelf.

"What's that?" Zoe asked.

"Mashed potatoes."

"For the doughnuts?"

"Yup."

"I don't want your doughnuts," Zoe said as she rolled over onto her side and closed her eyes.

I know. I know. Mashed potato doughnuts? Sounds even crazier than olive oil ice cream. But Mom had told me once that if you substitute mashed potatoes for some of the flour, they'll make whatever you're baking lighter. Winnie's doughnuts were awesome, but I wanted mine fluffier, and I was going to use mashed potatoes to do it. Mom's mashed potatoes were just potato. This was for Jeanine, who was always complaining about how Mom had to "fancy" everything up. Mom made them every week, and we always had a ton of leftovers. If this worked, I figured I could just chip in for potatoes.

So, as Zoe napped on the kitchen floor, I mapped out a new recipe.

After an hour of thinking and looking through cookbooks, I had a plan. I'd come up with three new ingredients: mashed potatoes for the dough and balsamic vinegar and instant coffee (no caffeine) for the chocolate cream. Since the doughnut was so sweet, I wanted to make the cream less sweet, more chocolaty. One of the cookbooks said a little balsamic vinegar gives chocolate a stronger flavor. The coffee was a trick I'd seen Mom use when she doesn't want milk chocolate to taste too sweet. The instant stuff just dissolves so it's easy to use. I'd have to be careful not to put in too much though, or I'd end up with mocha cream doughnuts.

I made three small batches of dough. In the first one, I used mashed potatoes for half of the flour, then in the second, I used it for only a third, and in the last one, just a quarter.

While the dough was rising, I experimented with the cream. On their own, the vinegar and the coffee gave the chocolate exactly what I was going for, but together, they made it a bit bitter. In the end, I chose the coffee because I liked the way it upped the cocoa flavor.

Once I'd fried and rolled the doughnuts, I tasted one from each batch. The winner was obvious. It was by far the lightest. It had the same yummy flavor as Winnie's, but it tasted more like cake. Since mashed potatoes were supposed to make the doughnuts lighter, it surprised me that the lightest one had the smallest amount of potato. It just goes to show you that in cooking, more isn't always better. That meant I'd just need one cup of mashed potatoes per batch, which would be easy to swing even if I ended up having to make them myself.

By the time I was ready to start stuffing, it was getting dark and Zoe was just waking up from her marathon nap.

"Feel better?" I said.

She rolled onto her side and sat up. "I'm hungry."

I wasn't surprised. It had been almost two hours since she'd eaten the doughnuts, and I'd forgotten to feed us lunch. We were both in need of some real food.

Minutes later, we were eating leftover chicken looking out the window at rabbits playing freeze tag on the front lawn. Something you may not know: rabbits are seriously good freezers.

"Did you really put mashed potato in the doughnuts?" Zoe asked, pointing to the empty bowl with her chicken leg.

"Yup, and they're awesome."

Zoe swore she wouldn't even taste my doughnuts, but she did want to stuff them. She was super into the pastry gun. So, when we'd finished our chicken and washed our hands, I spooned my new cream into the gun and let her fill the three doughnuts I had left from the winning batch. When she'd stuffed them all, she held one up and studied it as if she'd be able to spot the part with mashed potato and eat around it.

This time, I couldn't wait to taste my creation. I knew the cream was mind-blowing, and I knew the doughnuts were mind-blowing, but how would they be together? Had I made something entirely new like PB&J or just some D stuffed with some C?

I picked up a doughnut and knocked it gently into the one Zoe was still inspecting. "Cheers!"

The lighter, cakier doughnut floated for a second on my tongue, then melted into the chocolate…

I'd done it!

Because the chocolate was more rich than sweet, my taste buds craved more doughnut. The doughnut and the cream worked together in a way they hadn't before. This wasn't just some D plus some C. It was picture-in-the-paper and get-up-at-dawn and flying-carpet just like it had been before. It was all those things, and it was mine and it was Winnie's and it was life changing.

I guess after seeing the look on my face, Zoe couldn't hold out any longer because she finally nibbled at the doughnut. As she chewed, her eyes opened a little wider, and before she'd even swallowed the first bite, she took another one that got her all the way to the chocolate. Her eyes rolled back a few seconds later, and she made this sound that was part giggle and part sigh, like this doughnut, my doughnut, was something she'd been missing forever and finally found.

"Let's put mashed potatoes in everything!" she said and sucked chocolate off her thumb with a loud smack.

After that, I was so full of *Shazzam,* I agreed to help Zoe clean up the basement. I even promised not to tell my parents about the mess she'd made.

I was just lugging the vacuum cleaner up from the basement when I heard Mom calling me. She was standing at the top of the stairs, still in her bathrobe but looking less green than before.

"I think I could manage some ginger ale. Bring me some?" she called down.

"Sure."

I told Zoe I'd be back in a second, got the ginger ale, and headed upstairs.

I guess I did take longer than a second, because Mom and I got to talking about how the D turned out, and by the time I got back to kitchen, Zoe was gone. So was the pastry gun.

I found them both in Jeanine's room. The gun was empty.

"Okay, where's the cream?" I hoped she could hear how annoyed I was and that she'd actually care.

She grinned. Not a chance.

"You're gonna be so sick." I'd assumed she'd eaten all the cream. That's what I would have done.

"No, I'm not." She rocked from one foot to the other. "I like stuffing things."

"Things? Like doughnuts?"

Her eyes moved slowly from one side of the room to the other. "And other things."

"Things like that?" I pointed to Jeanine's model of the human heart. I thought I'd caught her eyes stop at it for a second too long as she looked around the room.

She shook her head but smiled bigger.

"What about that?" I was pointing to the inflatable space shuttle next to it.

"Uh-uh."

"Come on, Zoe. Give it up. Where's the cream?"

"No, this is fun. Keep trying," she said, jumping up and down.

I didn't have time for this. I was just about to yell for my mother when I noticed Paws, Jeanine's bear, was on the desk and not on her pillow where she always left him.

"Please tell me you didn't." I reached for the bear.

Paws felt like he'd gained a few pounds and was disturbingly squishy. I gave him a little squeeze, and something dribbled out onto the floor.

Zoe clapped.

That was it. Enough. I'd done my best. My mother was off the bathroom floor. My shift was over.

I snatched the pastry gun out of Zoe's hands, dragged her and Paws into my parents' room, showed Paws's new trick to my mother, and then went back downstairs.

In case you're wondering, no, there is no way to clean chocolate cream from the inside of a teddy bear. Mom found this place in Nebraska though that can completely remake stuffed animals with new insides, so in six weeks Paws was back, even better than new. Zoe lost her Dessert Days for the entire time he was undergoing reconstructive surgery, but I'm pretty sure she'd tell you it was worth it and that she'd do it again if she got the chance. Just in case, we keep the pastry gun under tight security now.

19

A few days after Doughnut Day, I woke to Mom shouting, "I thought we were done with this!"

I leaned over the side of my bed and peeked through the hole in the floor. Mom, Jeanine, and Zoe were standing in a circle right under my room staring at something I couldn't see on the hall carpet.

"Zoe, I don't even know what to say," Mom said.

Since whatever it was, it wasn't my fault, I put the pillow over my head and tried to go back to sleep.

It was no use. Josh's voice was playing on a loop in my head: "Why should *you* invest in the Doughnut Stop? The *real* question is: How can you afford not to?"

They were lines from our investor presentation. We'd rehearsed for hours the day before because we were pitching my parents that morning. Before we'd practiced though, I'd come clean about how I'd made Winnie's recipe my own. Then I'd made Josh taste a doughnut I'd made from the original recipe and a new one and told him that if he didn't like the new one better, we'd go with the original. Luckily, the new doughnuts tasted a lot like yellow cake with chocolate frosting, which I now know is Josh's favorite, so there was no contest. If you like breadier, heavier doughnuts—and there's nothing wrong with those—you'd probably have gone for the original. But the Doughnut Stop's specialty is the light, cakey doughnut.

"There's just one problem," Josh had said after he'd wolfed down the doughnut.

I knew exactly where he was going. "Winnie."

"We have to tell her," he said.

"I know. And if she doesn't like it, I kind of feel like we have to use the original recipe unless we want to make completely different doughnuts, and I don't want to do that because the whole point was bringing the chocolate cream doughnut back to Petersville."

"So I guess we just tell her and pray she's okay with it."

"But we don't have to tell her like now or anything." I wasn't prepared to deal with Winnie yet.

"Nope. No rush." Josh clearly wasn't either.

When Josh and I were preparing for our investor presentation, I told him everything my dad had taught me about making a good pitch. Josh was now a word-punching master. All his lines had these tunes you couldn't get out of your head like commercials on TV. I'd tried to convince him to do the whole pitch on his own, but he wouldn't go for it. He said I had to do it with him because the Doughnut Stop was my idea, and investors would want to see the brains behind the operation. In this case, since our only potential investors were *my* parents, I had to agree with him.

Even with me doing half the pitch, I still wasn't sure my parents would come through. I know what you're thinking: the project was their idea. How could they not support you after you did all that work? That's what Josh thought too. And it's not that I didn't see that. I did. But they'd said some things that worried me. Things like, "Tris, even if the doughnut stand never happens, think how much you've learned from this process!" Like I'd been playing a round of Life as the doughnut business guy and wasn't that a lot of fun. They didn't get that this wasn't just a game I was wasting time playing till school started. Maybe that's how it had begun, but it wasn't like that anymore. Now I was building something real, an actual business with real doughnuts for real people, chocolate-cream-doughnut-starved people.

I got out of bed, put on my good pants, a button-down shirt, and my only tie. Josh and I had decided to dress up to show my parents how serious we were, and also because the book says you have to dress for success.

It must have been a while since I'd worn my good pants, because as I climbed down the ladder, there was a loud, ripping sound. I waited for somebody to laugh, but nobody even looked up.

"I'm just so disappointed in you," I heard Mom say as I climbed the rest of the way down.

"But I didn't do it," Zoe said, stomping her dress-up Cinderella heels.

"It's just gross," Jeanine said. "And it means you're still a baby."

"I'm not a baby. It's not mine. Look at it. It doesn't even look like mine."

Jeanine and Mom bent over and studied whatever it was on the floor.

"What are we looking at?" I said, peering over Jeanine. "Oh."

There, on the hall carpet, was a sizable pile of poop.

"She does have a point," I said.

"What do you mean?" Mom said.

"It *doesn't* look like hers."

"How would you know? Have you been studying her poops?" Jeanine asked.

"No, I haven't been studying her poops," I said, giving Jeanine a dirty look.

Would it kill her to stick up for Zoe? I mean, what did I know? Maybe Zoe had taken a poop right there in the middle of the upstairs hall, and yeah, it was completely disgusting, but Zoe didn't need Jeanine on her case too. That was Mom's job. "She just never flushes the toilet," I explained.

Zoe doesn't like the flush. She doesn't trust it will be satisfied with sucking down only what's in the bowl, so when she does flush, which is only when my parents make her, she quickly pulls the lever and takes off like she's just lit a stick of dynamite.

Just then, my father came up the stairs. "So, *this* is where the party is."

"Zoe pooped on the floor, and now she's lying about it," Jeanine said.

Zoe stomped on Jeanine's foot with the Cinderella shoe. "I did not!"

Jeanine screamed.

"Let me see, honey," Mom said, bending over to examine Jeanine's foot. "You're okay. Go put some ice on it."

"What happened to using our words, Zo?" Dad said. "Say, 'sorry.'"

"Sorry."

"That's it? You're not going to punish her?"

"What were you looking for? Firing squad, guillotine perhaps?"

"She broke my toe!"

"So the guillotine then," Dad said. "Come on, Zo Zo. We're going to chop off your head."

Zoe giggled.

"What kind of a message do you think you send by turning this into a joke?"

"Just go get some ice, Jeanine," Mom said.

Jeanine made a face and staggered off down the hall.

"Now, what are we going to do about *this*?" Mom pointed at the poop.

Dad squatted and studied it. Then he scooped Zoe up and leaned his forehead against hers. "Zo Zo, is that your poop?"

"No."

"Is it Tawatty Tawatty Dabu Dabu's poop?" I asked.

"I told you, they're gone."

"All right then." My father put Zoe down.

"All right then, what?" Mom said.

Dad raised an *aha* finger. "What we have here is a case of mystery poop."

"Tom." Mom rolled her eyes. "Would you please pretend to be an adult?"

"Don't worry. The kids and I are on the case. Right, guys?" he said, bouncing his eyebrows up and down at us.

"Don't look at me. I've got work to do," I said.

"Then would my two remaining turd detectives start with cleaning it up, and would whoever left it, please not do it again?" Mom said.

She so still thought it was Zoe's.

When I got down to the kitchen, Jim the Kidnapper/Carpenter was sitting at the table drinking coffee out of Mom's "Number One Mom" mug.

"Oh, hi," I said.

"Morning," Jim said.

"I thought my dad said the roof was done."

"It is, Jax," Jim said, winking at me. He never told my parents about that day he picked me up in the flood, but he called me Jax every now and then just to show me he remembered, which felt like a typical, creepy kidnapper move.

"So, what are you doing here?" I said.

"Tris!" Mom yelled from the top of the stairs. "'What are you doing here?' Really?"

"Sorry," I said more to her than to Jim. It was weird the way he was just sitting there drinking his coffee in our kitchen like he belonged there. Why did I have to play host?

"No apology necessary. You were curious. Curiosity is useful. Certainly more useful than manners," Jim said, winking again.

"Thanks," I said, though I wasn't at all sure he'd meant what he'd said as a compliment. The wink had thrown me. Usually, a wink means the winker and winkie have a secret, like when he'd called me Jax. But what did this wink mean? It could have meant: both you and I know that asking a direct question isn't offensive even if your mother doesn't. But then it also could have meant: both you and I know that you're just a rude kid, and I'm making fun of you for it.

"I'm actually here for you," Jim said and then took a swig of coffee. "Winnie told me about your doughnut business."

"She did?"

I hadn't expected Winnie to be talking up the doughnuts around town, but it was great news that she was. *Starting Your Own Business for Dummies* says the best kind of advertising is word-of-mouth because it's free and creates something called buzz.

"Yeah, so she wanted me to get the process rolling on your business license." He leaned forward and pulled a square of folded paper out of the back pocket of his jeans.

"Business license? For a little stand."

"If you're selling stuff, you need a license."

This had to be some kind of joke he and Winnie had cooked

up. No way a kid needed a business license, but I decided to play along. "Okay, let's say you're right. Let's say I need a business license. What's that got to do with you?"

"As mayor, I'm on the Chamber of Commerce," he said, his beard stretching wide with his smile.

Of course! Jim the Kidnapper/Carpenter was also the mayor. How had I not seen that coming? Jim the Kidnapper was the mayor, and a twelve-year-old trying to sell doughnuts on the street out of a cardboard box needed a business license.

This wasn't a joke. This was Petersville.

"Yeah, been almost five years now. Truth is nobody else wants the job, and I'm not too bad at it." Jim thumped his belly like the extra pounds in there had something to do with his success.

"Okay, fine. I give up. You're the mayor, and I need a business license. Can you just tell me what I need to do to get this done as fast as possible?"

All I really cared about was that this wasn't going to slow us down. We had a timeline: get funding; order ingredients; create buzz; grand opening. We didn't have time for paperwork.

"You just need to present your business plan to the Chamber of Commerce."

That minute, the front door swung open, and Josh burst through holding a gigantic, stuffed...thing. It looked like something you'd win at a carnival, big and colorful and useless. It was almost as tall as he was, and THE DOUGHNUT STOP was stitched across it in red letters.

"Wow," I said. "That's...one big pillow."

"It's a doughnut," Josh grumbled.

"Oh, right, sorry. Now I see it," I said.

"I know. I know. I told her not to, but she felt bad that she doesn't have money to invest, so she did this."

"Your mom?" I asked.

He nodded. "I think she stayed up all night making it. I couldn't not take it."

"I get it," I said. Not just what it meant about his mom, but what it meant about him.

"I like it," Jim said, cocking his head to one side and studying the doughnut.

"You do?" Josh turned it around to look at the front of it.

"It would be great advertising if we can figure out the right place to put it," I said.

"We could strap it to the front of my truck," Jim suggested as he combed his fingers through his beard.

I laughed.

"I'm being serious," he said.

"Really?" I said.

"Sure."

"What's the catch?"

"No catch."

"But you'll want us to pay you, right?" He was offering to let us use his truck as a billboard. Of course he'd want something in return.

Jim shook his head.

"I don't understand. Why would you do that?"

"Why not?" he said with a shrug.

I didn't say anything. I'd never met a "why not?" person before. In the city, there's generally more of a "why should I?" kind of vibe.

"Thanks so much," Josh said, appreciative, but not at all surprised. He must have seen this "why not" thing before.

"Yeah, thanks," I said. "That would be great. Talk about buzz. A giant doughnut strapped to the front of the mayor's car is sure to get people excited."

"Now we just need to get this business license squared away." Jim tapped the folded-up paper.

"What business license?" Josh said. "Aren't we doing the investor pitch now?"

Suddenly, I had an idea about how to get Jim what he needed for the license and stay on schedule.

"We're actually presenting our business plan to my parents this morning," I said to Jim. "What if you just stayed for that? Then you could get all the information you need for the license."

"Sounds good to me. Just gotta make sure Harley can get over here."

"Harley?" I said.

"Harley Turnby. He's the other half of the Chamber of Commerce. In fact, if we don't agree, he's the deciding vote."

This seemed like good news. How tough could getting a business license be if Mr. Turnby of Turnby's Random Emporium was in charge?

"Hey, Jax, can I make a suggestion? Before Harley gets here, go change your pants." He pointed to my butt. "I don't much care, but Harley's kind of old school."

"Oh, right. Thanks." I quickly untucked my shirt and pulled it down in back.

Jim was no less creepy, but I had to appreciate a mayor who wasn't going to hold flashing my Knicks boxers through a hole in my chinos against me, not to mention a mayor who was going to strap a six-foot doughnut to the front of his truck just because he couldn't think of a reason not to.

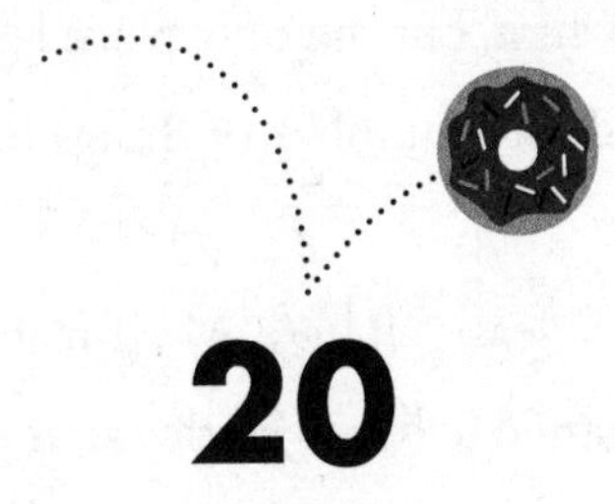

20

Normally, I think anyone wearing a bow tie looks just like Orville Redenbacher, the guy on the popcorn box, but when Harley Turnby came through our door, which, by the way, required him to duck and turn sideways, the Michelin tire man is who popped into my head. It didn't surprise me that someone who sells the Flowbee (a haircutting attachment for your vacuum cleaner) didn't know that bow ties look ridiculous, but I couldn't understand why Harley didn't get that they were health hazards for someone his size. The bow tie was clearly strangling him. His face was bright red, and his neck exploded in sweaty rolls out of his shirt collar.

"Doughnuts, huh?" Harley said when he'd finally made it through the door.

"Uh, yeah, doughnuts," I said and led him to the living room where everyone else was already waiting. I looked around for somewhere to park him, but the only place left was a stool, which he could have used for a number of things but a seat wasn't one of them.

Mom stood up. "Please, sit here, Mr. Turnby."

"Thanks," I mouthed to her as Harley squeezed himself into the armchair she'd been sitting in.

"Ready?" Josh called from a corner of the room.

Harley took a small spiral notebook and pen from his shirt pocket.

"Ready," I said.

The room went dark.

Zoe clapped. "Is there popcorns?"

"Is that really necessary?" Jeanine snapped. She was on the couch studying for the State Solve-a-Thon. Both she and Kevin had cleaned up at regionals.

"If you want light, go in the kitchen," my mother said.

Jeanine got up and stomped out of the room.

"Where's the popcorns?!"

"Shhh, it's not a movie," Dad said. "This is for Tris's doughnuts."

"So there are doughnuts?"

"No. There's no food. Quiet."

Josh switched on the projector his mom had lent us, and our first slide popped up on the sheet we'd hung on the wall:

The Doughnut Stop: What is it?
A doughnut stand on Main Street in Petersville that will operate on Saturday and Sunday mornings from 8:00 a.m. till we sell out.

Josh went first. He read the slide, then explained how we were going to limit each customer to two doughnuts. I'd come up with that after I'd read that a good way to keep demand high when you're starting out is to keep your supply low, like limited edition sneakers.

"So doughnuts, huh?" Harley said again. This seemed a little weird since he'd asked the same thing five minutes before, but I figured he just wanted to make sure Josh and I were on the same page.

"That's right, doughnuts," Josh said.

"Doughnuuuts," Harley repeated slowly as he wrote on his little pad.

"We'll probably increase our numbers over time but—"

"What about candy necklaces?" Harley interrupted.

"What about them?" I said.

"You gonna sell those?"

"Uh, no, no candy necklaces," I said.

"No caaannndyyy nnecklaaces," Harley repeated as he wrote.

Josh finished his lines, then flipped to the next slide:

Why is the Doughnut Stop guaranteed to succeed?

Simple: Winnie Hammond's famous chocolate cream doughnuts have a devoted following. This product will draw customers from miles around.

After I read the slide, I did my lines about how people had gone crazy for Winnie's doughnuts. I was just about to quote from the article when Harley said, "So, it's not just any doughnuts then. It's only chocolate cream doughnuts. Is that what I'm hearing?"

"That's right," I said.

"So no old-fashioneds or glazed or sprinkle?"

"Nope." Harley was beginning to get on my nerves.

"Noooo olllld-faaaasheeeoooned, glaaaa—"

"Okay, Josh. Next slide, please." Harley's questions were really messing with our flow.

Why should you invest in the Doughnut Stop?

- Great return on your investment.
- Give doughnuts back to the community.

Before Josh had even finished reading the slide, Harley was at it again.

"And what about Chinese checkers?"

"No! Of course not. Just doughnuts!" I'd completely lost my cool. "What's going on here?" I said, turning on the lights. If I'd let things go on like that, Harley would have ruined the whole pitch.

"I'm going to put everything you're not going to sell on the business license. That way, if you sell anything you're not supposed to, we can shut you down," Harley explained.

"Oh no!" Jeanine yelled from the kitchen. A second later, she was standing over Harley wagging a finger at him. "I know what you're doing."

"What's he doing?" I asked.

"He's trying to keep you from selling anything he sells at his store."

"Oh. But we don't want to sell anything he sells. Really," I said to Harley.

"That's not the point!" Jeanine said. "The point is you can sell anything you want. That's your right."

"No. *That's* not the point," I argued. "We only want to sell doughnuts. That's what this is about."

"But you can't let him refuse to give business licenses to people unless they promise not to sell anything that he might. He's trying to stop people from competing with him."

"I'm so sorry, Mr. Turnby." Mom grabbed Jeanine's pointing finger and forced it down. "Jeanine, I'm sure that's not what he's doing."

"Oh, no, that's what I'm doing," Harley said, nodding. "But if these boys promise they're just going to sell chocolate cream doughnuts, there's no problem."

"No problem? No problem?" shrieked Jeanine. "You know what you are? You're a monopolist!"

"I am?" A smile exploded on Harley's face. He clearly knew about as much as I did about what a monopolist was.

"You can't keep people from selling the products you sell so you can force them to buy from you. It's illegal! And un-American!" Jeanine looked like she was seconds away from whipping out her Future Lawmakers of America badge and making a citizen's arrest.

"I can't?" Harley looked around like he suddenly didn't know where he was. "Jim?"

"Technically, it's a no-no, Harley," Jim said. "This is actually Harley's first term, so he's still learning. Jax, you want to sell candy necklaces or Flowbees, you go right ahead. You got my blessing and the license too. Right, Harley?"

Harley shrugged his shoulders. "I guess. I mean, if I have to."

"Thanks, but I think we'll stick to chocolate cream doughnuts," I said.

"But now you don't have to," Jeanine said, flashing her *Yes, I won!* smile at Harley.

"Fine," I said. "Can we get back to the pitch now?"

"Fine? Don't you mean thanks?" she said, her smile caving in to a big black hole of what's-wrong-with-you.

I could have tried to explain that Josh and I would have been perfectly happy promising never to sell anything but chocolate cream doughnuts even if it did violate the Constitution, but I knew that would have taken too long.

"Right. I meant thanks," I said.

Then we turned out the light and started from the beginning, and this time everything went perfectly. Nobody interrupted, and at the end, not only did my parents decide to invest but so did Jim and Harley.

By the time I went to tell Winnie we had the money that afternoon, I'd started to wonder why people had invested. Did they really think the Doughnut Stop would succeed, or had they given us money just to be nice?

"People don't give you money just to be nice, especially when people is Harley Turnby," Winnie said.

That should have made me happy. It meant people believed us

when we said the Doughnut Stop was guaranteed to be a hit. The problem was, we didn't actually know that, not for sure.

So what happened if we were wrong?

What happened if we couldn't even make enough money to pay them back? What if the business was a complete and total flop? What if we were the Flowbee of the doughnut world? We'd promised Harley Turnby we'd make his money back and then some. What would he do to us if it turned out we'd lied?

I knew where to go for answers: the only twenty-seven pages of *Starting Your Own Business for Dummies* I hadn't read…Chapter 19: Bankruptcy. It seemed like a jinx to read about what happens when your business goes belly up, so I'd just skipped that part.

But now I wanted to know. Now I had to know.

Just in case.

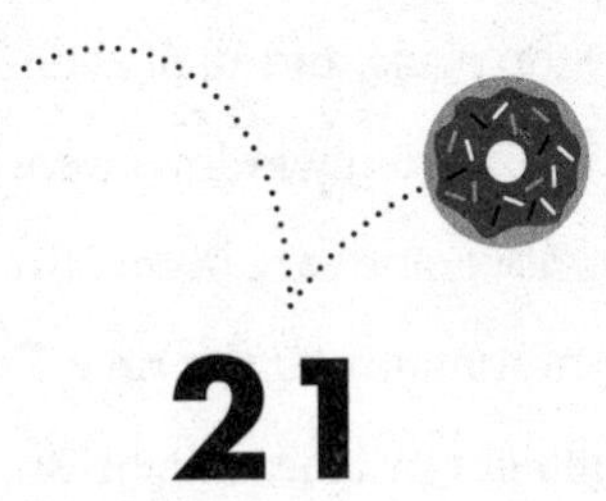

21

My parents had all kinds of rules when we lived in the city: never take a shortcut through a parking lot; never take the subway by yourself; and if someone tries to take your stuff, just let them have it. But since I'd gotten to Petersville, my parents had given me just one rule: no biking after dark.

At first, I didn't get it. What did I need the rule for? Why exactly would I *want* to be riding around in the dark? Then the clocks changed and it started getting dark at four in the afternoon, and the rule didn't seem so dumb anymore.

Since I didn't have school or really anywhere I had to be, I'd stopped paying much attention to what time it was. I'd even stopped wearing my watch. The afternoons Josh and I spent skating on the pond, it didn't matter how late it got since he always stayed for dinner and his mom just picked him up afterward. The problem was when he and I were hanging out at the library. We'd be sitting there making Doughnut Stop plans, and all of a sudden, I'd notice that the bookshelves opposite the front windows were lit up all orange. Then I'd jump up, yell goodbye, and race home. Even though the sun was usually behind the mountains by the time I got there, the sky just above them was still light or at least light-ish, which I thought was good enough. If my parents disagreed, they never said so.

The thing is, there are no windows in the little office behind the circulation desk, and that's where Josh and I met Winnie two days before the Doughnut Stop's grand opening. We'd *told* her we had to meet that afternoon to work out some stuff for the opening. The *real* reason for the meeting? We were finally going to tell her I'd messed with her recipe. That's not how I saw it, but I was pretty sure that's how she would.

"Oh, good, snacks," Winnie said when she came through the door. "I think better on a full stomach."

I'd made a batch of doughnuts using the new recipe and arranged some on a paper plate in the center of the table.

"You roll 'em right after you take 'em out of the oil, right?"

"Uh-huh," I said.

"Because it looks like you were being a little stingy with the sugar on these, Slick. Don't do that this weekend."

"I won't."

"Don't forget."

"He won't," Josh said.

"Maybe he should write it down to make sure."

"Uh, okay." I looked around for something to write with and on.

"I got it," Josh said, writing in his Doughnut Stop binder. "Why don't you just tell Winnie about the…um…your news?"

"What news?" Winnie reached for a doughnut.

"No!" Before I knew what I was doing, I'd snatched the plate out from under her hand.

"What? Those just for decoration?"

"I need to tell you something first."

"I can eat while you talk. They call it multitasking."

"Actually…" Josh pushed the plate back across the table. "Maybe she should taste a doughnut first."

I shot Josh a look.

"What's wrong with you boys?" Winnie picked up a doughnut and took a big bite.

I squeezed the edge of the table and held my breath.

"Mmm. Mmm."

"Good, huh?" Josh said.

"'Course, they're good."

"They don't taste…a little different?" I said.

"From other doughnuts? Yeah, a lot better." She laughed.

"No. I mean, from before."

She took another bite and chewed slowly. "I haven't made my doughnuts for more than a year, Slick. But these are them."

The pressure was killing me. I just had to say it and get it over with. "I changed the recipe!"

"What are you talking about? You don't think I know my own doughnuts."

"They're *still* your doughnuts. I didn't change much. I just added a little mashed potato and instant coffee."

Winnie looked at her doughnut. "You expect me to believe there's mashed potato and coffee in here."

"There is. I'm serious."

"O-kay, Slick. Whatever you say. Maybe some chili peppers in here too?" She took another big bite.

"He's not kidding," Josh said.

"You know how I know you couldn't have changed my recipe?"

"How?"

"Because anything different would be worse. And these are just too good," she said as she helped herself to another one.

And just like that, what was right and what was wrong got all mixed up. It hadn't felt right not to tell Winnie what I'd done, but now that I had, it didn't feel right to make her believe it. I just knew she'd think I'd changed the recipe because I didn't think it was good enough and that wasn't true. Not even close.

I gave Josh a now-what look.

"Uh, I just remembered something," Josh said. "My mom wanted us to move some books. We'll be back in a second. C'mon, Tris."

"Take your time. I've got my doughnuts for company."

I followed Josh out of the room and into the computer nook.

"We have to let it go," he whispered.

"I know. That's what I was thinking. Does that make us liars?"

"No. We *tried* to tell her," he said. "I'm just worried that if we make her believe it, she'll think we thought there was something wrong with her doughnuts."

"I know, but there wasn't. Maybe I should just go back to using the recipe like it was."

"Why? She *loves* these doughnuts. *We* love these doughnuts. Plus, she thinks they're the exact same ones she was making anyway. What's she going to think if you go back to the other recipe?"

"She'll realize we were telling the truth, that these are different, and then...probably think I didn't like the doughnuts the way she made them."

"Right. She'll feel..."

"Bad," I said.

"Really bad."

"Okay, so we agree. We'll let it go, but not because we were too chicken to tell her the truth."

"Right," Josh said. "We told her. We just don't want to make her feel bad by making her believe it."

"Right. And everyone's—"

"You boys done whispering yet." Winnie's head popped up from behind a computer monitor.

I jumped. "Sorry. We were just..."

"About to come back," Josh said.

"Don't bother. I ate all the doughnuts. I'm going home to get some Pepto," she said. "See you Saturday, bright and early." It was only then as I watched Winnie walk out of the library that I realized that the sun had already moved all the way down the bookshelves.

"Oh no! What time is it?"

"After four thirty. Call your parents and tell them my mom will drop you off after closing."

I felt bad asking Josh's mom to drive just because I couldn't keep track of time. "Nah. I can make it."

And I did, but just. Only a thin band of light blue was still above the mountains when I reached the driveway.

I ditched my bike in the bushes at the bottom of Terror Mountain because I was too winded to drag it up. And even without it, the hike took forever. After blasting my legs biking home, they felt so heavy, it was as if I had bricks loaded on my feet.

"I'm here! I'm here!" I jumped up and down, waving my arms as I came out of the woods onto the lawn. My mother was at the kitchen window, and she waved. She must have heard me, but it was definitely too dark to see me by now. She didn't look like she was mad. She didn't look like she'd even noticed it was getting dark.

Safe!

I dropped to the ground and lay there in the dead leaves, breathing hard.

"Tris!"

It sounded like Jeanine, but I couldn't see her. I sat up and looked back at the house. My mother wasn't at the window anymore, and the front door was still closed.

"Tris!"

"Jeanine?" I stood up and looked around.

"Up here!" Something rustled high in the branches of a tall, nearby tree. I walked over to its base and looked up. In one of the highest branches, I could just make out the shape of a person.

"*What* are you doing?"

Jeanine made a loud, long, snot-slurping sound. "I'm stuck."

"Are you okay?"

"No! I'm stuck."

"I meant, are you hurt?"

"Like physically?"

"Yeah, like are you too hurt to climb down?"

I listened for an answer. "Jeanine?"

"I got a scratch on my hand!"

"And you can't climb down?"

She didn't answer.

"Jeanine?"

Still nothing.

"Jeanine, did you try to climb down?"

"I can't. I told you. I'm stuu—" Her last word was eaten up by loud sobs.

"You're not stuck. You're just scared."

The sobs got louder.

I looked back at the house. Mom was afraid of heights, and she hadn't even let Dad climb a stepladder since his concussion.

"Okay, Jeanine. Just hang on." I reached up, grabbed onto a thick branch with both hands, jammed a foot in the groove where the trunk met the branch, and pulled myself up.

Climbing that tree was actually easier than climbing the rope ladder up to my room. Unlike a rope ladder, a tree does you the favor of standing still. Also, unlike other trees, this one had branches in just the right places so you never had to stretch too far.

"This tree is awesome," I called when I was about halfway up.

"It scored highest for climbability."

I laughed. "You ranked the trees."

"I studied branch spacing and thickness to determine best climbability."

"Of course you did," I said to myself.

In no time, I was straddling a branch on the opposite side of the trunk from Jeanine.

"Cool view," I said. Sky was all around us. It was darker now, and a few stars had already popped out.

"Oh, yeah?"

I peered around the trunk and squinted at her. "Are your eyes closed?"

"Uh-huh."

"I think I know how to get you unstuck."

"I'm *not* opening my eyes."

"Jeanine." I laughed.

"This isn't funny! Can you please just help me?"

"I'm trying, but you have to open your eyes."

"If I open my eyes, you're going to make me climb down."

"That is the goal, isn't it?"

"What if I can't?"

"Then we'll get a crane."

"I mean it." She squeezed the trunk tighter.

I thought for a minute. Climbing down was the big goal, but maybe I could start her on a small one. "Don't think about going down yet. Just open your eyes and see how cool it is up here."

"Just open my eyes? That's it?"

"That's it. Just open your eyes and tell me what the really bright star right over our heads is."

She was quiet for a bit. "It's not one star. It's four."

"Really?"

"Yeah, it's Capella. Two giant yellow stars and two red dwarves."

"It's super bright."

"Yeah, it is pretty," she said like she didn't like admitting it. "You know, I hate it out here, but I love how you can see the stars. That's *one* thing you can't do at home."

Home was still somewhere else for Jeanine.

For a while, we sat there, not talking, looking up the sky. I kept covering one eye and trying to see the four different stars in that one bright light, but it was impossible.

"Hey, can I ask you a question?" I said.

"I'm not climbing down."

"I know. I know. Relax. I just want to know why you climbed up in the first place."

"I don't know."

"Come on. Yes, you do. You plan everything. You even ranked the tree for climbability."

"It's dumb. It's too dumb."

"I do dumb stuff all the time."

"But I don't."

"I hate to break it to you, but, yeah, you do. It's just a different kind of dumb stuff."

She took a deep breath and blew it out hard. "Fine. Mom got a call from Waydin Elementary, you know, just about stuff for when we start school, and it got me thinking about the kids here and how they're gonna to think I'm, you know, weird."

"Uh-huh."

"Thanks."

"Sorry. I just meant, 'Uh-huh, I'm listening, keep going,' not, 'Uh-huh, you *are* weird.'"

"Anyway, I was looking out the window, and I just started thinking about how I'd never climbed a tree. And how probably if you grew up around here, you'd have to, I mean you just would have, right? Like how could you grow up here and not? So I thought, I'm going to do it, just so I can be someone who's climbed a tree, so at least there'll be one thing about me that's not different."

"Okay."

"Anyway, it turned out to be super, super dumb."

"But just think about all the money you'll make selling your climbability formula to the other kids."

"That's not funny," she said, though I thought I heard her smiling against her will.

"Hey, you know, Josh and I were talking today about how if the Doughnut Stop does well, we may want to branch out to other flavors of cream. *Starting Your Own Business for Dummies* says customers get bored if you don't offer new product lines. Anyway, so I was thinking, it was good you made Harley say it was okay for us to sell things other than just *chocolate* cream doughnuts."

"See."

"Yeah, well, thanks."

"You're welcome."

Neither of us said anything for a while after that, and I began wondering if my parents were looking for us. Unlike when we used to live in the apartment, there were lots of places we could be in the house, and it could take a pretty long time before they thought it was strange that they hadn't seen us.

Finally, Jeanine peeked around the trunk and said, "I'm cold. I want to go home."

"You know the only way home is down, right?"

"I know. Can you, like, hold on to me somehow?"

"Like carry you? I don't think so."

"No, just hold on to me. So I know you're there."

It took me a while to come up with a system that worked, but eventually we were making our way down the tree. First, I'd lower myself to the next branch. Then I'd reach up and guide Jeanine's ankle to the branch I was holding on to. Since it was almost completely dark now, we had to feel our way from branch to branch.

When my feet finally reached the ground, I held Jeanine's hand and she jumped down. Then she did something that is not at all Jeanine: she hugged me. And not a quick hug—a long one, tight like she'd hugged the tree.

"Okay, let's go. I got to get back," she said, suddenly taking off for the house.

"What's the hurry?" I called after her.

"I just wasted like two hours up in that tree. The Solve-a-Thon's in five days!" When she reached the porch, she turned around. "Hey, what do you think of butterscotch?"

"For what?"

"Your next doughnut flavor. It's just an idea."

"I *love* butterscotch."

"I know," she said. "Why do you think I thought of it?"

"It's genius," I said and meant it.

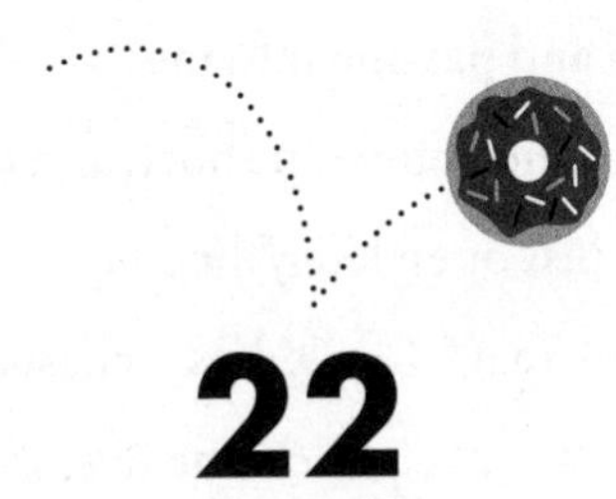

22

Here's one thing *Starting Your Own Business for Dummies* doesn't tell you: if you're not a morning person, don't start a doughnut business.

The doughnuts and I would have to be ready to leave the house by seven thirty if we were going to be set up on Main Street by eight o'clock. Even if I made the dough and the cream the night before, I'd still need at least two and half hours to cut, fry, roll, and fill all forty doughnuts. That meant getting up at four thirty in the middle of the night. I know, technically, it's morning then, but who are we kidding? If it's dark, it's still night, and no matter what kind of clock-changing is happening, it's always dark at four thirty.

"Can't you fry and fill the night before?" Josh said when I explained the problem. It was the day before our grand opening, and we were on the pond.

"No way. There's no point unless they're fresh," I said.

"I know, but four thirty? That's crazy," he said, sweeping the puck from the goal and passing it to me.

I put out my stick but came up short, and the puck flew by.

"Maybe we can just open later," he said.

"I thought about that," I called as I chased down the puck. "I don't think we can. It says eight on the flyers."

The flyers weren't fancy or anything. Josh had just taken a photo of a doughnut and put it next to a photo of Winnie giving a thumbs-up. Underneath it said, "Winnie's Famous Chocolate Cream Doughnuts at the Doughnut Stop, Main Street, Petersville. Come and Get 'Em! Saturdays and Sundays at 8:00 a.m., starting Saturday, December 20."

"Oh, yeah. It says so on the bumper stickers too," he said. "And who knows how many people have seen those by now."

Honk if you like chocolate cream doughnuts! and *I* ***stop*** *for the Doughnut Stop!* were everywhere. Winnie was giving them away at the General Store. Clive, her brother, was in the printing business.

We had serious buzz. Changing the time was not an option.

"It's fine," I said. "I'll just go to sleep really early. You know, like seven thirty."

"Yeah, as long as you get the same amount of sleep, it shouldn't matter what time you're getting up, right?"

"Right," I said.

Wrong.

The problem was, I wasn't tired at seven thirty. Really, who over the age of five is? It was just too early. Plus, I was too excited and too afraid my alarm wouldn't go off, or that it would go off and I would just go right back to sleep. What kind of nuddy misses his own grand opening? Even if Josh made it, he wouldn't have anything to sell, and the book says if you let your customers down once, they won't give you a second chance.

I know I did finally fall asleep because when the alarm went off, I dreamed the beeping was the kitchen timer and that I couldn't reach it because I was stuck under a doughnut the size of an elephant. When I eventually woke up enough to realize that I wasn't actually stuck under an enormous baked good, I leaped out of bed.

Fear of failure must work a lot like caffeine does, but only if you care about the thing you might fail. I definitely never woke up feeling like I'd been sleep-guzzling Coke on days I had tests at school.

I'd left my clothes in a pile next to my bed, and in seconds, I was dressed and climbing down the ladder. Halfway down, I heard something scurrying around just below me.

"Zoe?"

Whoever it was took off down the hall.

"Hey, I don't care!" I whispered-yelled. I figured I'd caught her creeping into my parents' room again. Since we'd moved, she preferred sleeping under my parents' bed than in her own.

I climbed down the next couple of rungs and then jumped to the floor.

That's when I heard it, the Darth-Vader-phlegm-breathing from the other end of the hall:

"Cchhhhuuuu Whlluuuhhhh Cchhhhuuuu Whlluuuhhhh..."

I froze.

Unlike Darth Vader, whatever it was didn't sound calm. It sounded crazy angry, like rip-my-arms-and-legs-from-my-body angry.

If I'd been able to move, I would have run, but I was too scared. So I just stood there waiting to be wishboned.

But nothing happened, and suddenly, the noise stopped. When a minute had passed and it hadn't started again, I ran my hand along the wall till I felt the light switch and flipped it.

Just outside the bathroom was a raccoon the size of a Big Wheel.

I'm not sure what happened next. I may have screamed, but if I did, I don't think I managed to get much sound out because nobody came running. What I do remember is that for a while, we—me and the raccoon—just stared at each other, and the weird thing was he looked almost as surprised as I was, like this was his house and *I* had scared *him* on *his* way to the bathroom in the middle of the night.

As soon as I could get my legs to move, I ran to my parents' room at the opposite end of the hall, slammed the door behind me, and jumped onto their bed with both feet.

"Ow, my hair!" my mother screamed.

"Who is that?" Dad grabbed my foot.

"It's me." I dropped to my knees.

Dad sat up. "Tris? What is it?"

"A raccoon," I whispered, though I'm not sure who I was worried about hearing me.

"Where?" Mom said.

"Out there." I pointed to the door.

"Why?" She wasn't so awake.

"Really? A raccoon in the house?" I could almost hear Dad smiling in the dark. Of course. This was something different.

"Yes, really!" I said.

"Houses aren't airtight. It happens," Dad said like it was no big deal.

"It happens? This isn't a mouse! It's a raccoon, and he's bigger than Zoe!"

"Relax. We'll get someone to come set some traps," he said.

"Okay, so what are you waiting for?"

"How about daylight?"

"But I need to go downstairs *now*."

"So go."

"You want me to go out there by myself, unarmed?"

"He's not going to attack you," Dad said as he hunkered down under the comforter. "Raccoons are shy."

"How do *you* know?"

"I read it…somewhere."

Ah. I see. In addition to being a master handyman, made-up Petersville dad was also a wildlife expert. "He didn't look shy! He looked mad, really mad, like I'd invaded his territory. You should have heard this sound he made."

"You're bigger than he is," Mom said.

"Not by much."

"Stop exaggerating. You'll be fine," she said, snuggling up to my father.

"You guys aren't actually going back to sleep, are you?"

Uh, yeah, they were.

"What if he's rabid?" I said.

"Highly unlikely," said the wildlife expert, his eyes already closed.

"Fine! But I'm taking this with me," I said, grabbing *The Art of French Cooking*, the thousand-page cookbook Mom keeps on her nightstand.

Mom opened her eyes. "You gonna teach it to make coq au vin?"

"It's for protection."

"Sounds good." Her eyes were closed again. "Have fun."

"You guys are never going to forgive yourselves if that raccoon attacks me."

"Good night," Dad said.

Jeanine would have been able to get them out of bed, and for a second, I thought about waking her up so she could do just that. But then what? She'd probably make us evacuate the house till some official from the National Wildlife Federation got there. Who knew when I'd be able to get into the kitchen then?

I opened my parents' door and peered out into the hall.

The raccoon was gone—or at least gone somewhere I couldn't see him. He was probably in the bathroom, which was fine by me. I was prepared to let him go about his business so long as he let me go about mine. He could have the upstairs bathroom. I'd use the one next to the kitchen.

I stepped out into the hall, hugging *The Art of French Cooking,* and started for the stairs. The light was still on, and that made me feel a little better.

I'd just made it to Jeanine's door when I heard a flush, and Zoe raced out of the bathroom.

"What happened?" I said, dropping the book and grabbing her arm as she sped by.

"Mommy promised me new glitter glue if I flush," she said, breathing hard.

"Oh. Everything okay in there?"

"Yeah. Just number one."

"No, I mean, you didn't see anything…weird?"

She shook her head.

I'd really thought he was in the bathroom. That had, after all, been where he was heading. I picked up the book and marched past Zoe into the bathroom.

I peeked behind the bathroom door.

No raccoon.

I ripped open the shower curtain.

No raccoon.

Zoe, who'd followed me in there, threw up the toilet seat. "What are we doing?"

"Looking for a raccoon."

The second I heard the words come out of my mouth, I wanted to shove them back in. Zoe was scared of the flush and the blow-up rat. She wasn't going to be okay sharing the house with a rodent who weighed more than she did.

"Awww. Was he cute?"

"Huh?" I'd gotten so lucky. "Uh, sure, yeah. He looked really... cuddly."

"And he was just walking around?" she said, laughing.

"Yup. Just walking around like he owned the joint."

Zoe stopped giggling suddenly. "The mystery poop!"

"What?"

"On the rug, remember?" She ran back into the hall and jumped on the spot where the mystery poop had been.

"Oh right."

"I *told* you it wasn't mine."

"I know. I believed you," I reminded her.

"Jeanine didn't."

"Jeanine won't believe that it was a raccoon either."

"Can we take a picture?"

"Of what?"

"Of the raccoon, so Jeanine knows."

"Sure. If I see it again, and if I have a camera on me, I promise to take a picture, especially if I see it pooping in the hall."

"Thank you!" She threw her arms around my legs and squeezed.

"Uh, no problem."

We stood there for a few seconds like that, then she unhugged me, wrapped as much of her hand as would fit around mine, and said, "What do you wanna do now?"

Unlike my parents, Zoe wasn't going back to sleep with a raccoon on the loose, not even if it was the cute, cuddly kind.

23

If I'm telling the truth, I never would have gotten the doughnuts done on time if Zoe hadn't helped. She cut while I fried, filled, and rolled. She kept pestering to fill too, but I'd learned my lesson so she stuck to cutting, and when she was done, I put her in that big, cardboard box till the last doughnut was rolled and the pastry gun had been cleaned and put in a secure location.

At seven, my parents came downstairs.

"Isn't it beautiful?" Mom said.

"Isn't what beautiful?" I said as I boxed up the last doughnuts.

"The snow." Dad pointed to the window.

There had to be a foot of snow on the ground, and cotton-ball-size flakes were still floating down.

"No! No! No!" I shouted. We hadn't planned for snow.

"How could you have missed that?" Jeanine said as she came down the stairs.

"I don't know. It was dark before, and I was concentrating."

"On what?" she said.

"On doughnuts."

"They're doughnuts, not brain surgery," she said, opening a box.

"Don't even think about it!" I warned.

"Jeanine, leave your brother and his doughnuts alone," Dad said.

"I have to go to this doughnut stand opening, and I can't even get a doughnut?"

Jeanine was on a mission to make my parents regret forcing her to come to the Doughnut Stop's grand opening instead of letting her stay home to study for the Solve-a-Thon. Of course, the person who was really going to regret my parents' decision was me. I'd told them I didn't care if Jeanine came. And I really didn't. She and I were okay. But my parents said there was no way she could miss it. They said we all had to support each other. I tried to get them to see that even though they could force Jeanine to come, they couldn't actually force her to support me, but if you haven't noticed, parents like to pretend they can control things they can't.

"Tris maked believe he saw a raccoon," Zoe said to my father.

"Oh, that's right! I completely forgot you came in last night," he said.

"What *was* that about, honey?" Mom said.

"What *was* that about? It was about a raccoon in the house. Not a make-believe one. A real one. A very large, very real one."

"How would a raccoon even get inside?" Jeanine said.

"Good point," Dad said. "They're not like mice. They can't fit under doors. Okay, can anyone recall holding open the door for a raccoon? After you, Monsieur Raccoon."

Zoe giggled.

"Ha. Ha." So they didn't believe me. Let *them* bump into Monsieur Raccoon in the bathroom in the middle of the night. I hoped they did. They deserved it.

"It's just magical, isn't it?" Mom gazed out the window at the snow-covered trees. "It's like the world's been iced."

"Does everything have to be about food with you?" Jeanine said.

"This cannot be happening." I looked from the window to the doughnuts and back again.

"What did you think?" Jeanine said. "You're opening an outdoor stand in the middle of winter."

"I know. We just..." What could I say? I was a nuddy.

"Go ahead. Have one." I shoved the box at her. "Nobody's going to show up now anyway. What's the point?"

"Oh, no." Mom snatched the box. "You're going. Even if you've only got one customer."

"How will people even get there in this?"

"I'm sure there are plows out right now," Dad said. "And everyone around here has four-wheel drive and snow tires."

"I'm calling Josh," I said.

I went to the kitchen phone and dialed. There was no answer.

"See, he's already out in the snow waiting for you," Mom said. "Let's go."

She was right about one thing. Even if we didn't have customers, I couldn't let Josh down.

It was 7:44 on the digital car clock when we pulled up in front of Winnie's. Josh was supposed to have the card table set up there by then, but the table wasn't out and neither was he. Nobody was, and there wasn't a car in sight. Petersville was as dead as it had been that first morning, except now it was covered in snow.

"I'm telling you, Josh saw the snow and went back to sleep," Jeanine said.

"He wouldn't do that," I said, and I believed it. I did. But where was he?

"He probably thought nobody but a complete idiot would come out in a blizzard and try to sell doughnuts on a street corner," Jeanine said.

"Cut it out," Mom said.

"He would have called. He wouldn't just not show up," I said.

"So where is he then?" Jeanine said.

"Jeanine? Did you hear Mom? *Sa soofee!*" my father shouted.

That did it, and for a while the only sound in the car was the click-click of the blinkers as we sat there slowly disappearing under the snow.

"Look, don't those brighten up Main Street?" Mom pointed to flickering, white Christmas lights strung between the General Store and Renny's.

"Kinda weird," Jeanine said. "They're only on one side of the street."

"Maybe they just haven't finished putting them up," Mom said.

It was quiet again for a while. Then Jeanine said, "We should go."

"We're not going," Dad said.

"We're gonna get stuck," she sang to the tune of I-told-you-so. "The tires are already covered."

"We won't get stuck," Mom said.

"People die in blizzards like this. They starve, and they freeze," Jeanine said.

"I don't want to starve and freeze," Zoe said.

"Nobody's going to starve and freeze. This isn't even a blizzard. It's a little winter snow, and it's gorgeous," Dad said.

"A little winter snow? What do you call a hurricane? A little summer breeze?"

"If she wants to go, let her go!" I shouted, throwing open the car door. Then I climbed out and slammed it hard behind me.

If Josh wasn't going to show, if no one was going to show, I couldn't be in that car with them when I gave up.

"Tris, get back in!" Mom shouted out her window.

"Where are you going?" Dad called out his.

"Winnie's," I said, taking the doughnuts out of the trunk.

Winnie was all business. If it turned out nobody was coming, she wasn't going to feel bad for me. And no way would she put up with me feeling bad for myself. She'd make it about the doughnuts and the business, our business.

I was almost to Winnie's front door when something in her window made me stop. The sign. I'd seen it so many times I never even read it anymore, but the Christmas lights had been strung up on the outside of the window right around it so my eyes couldn't help themselves:

Yes, we really do have chocolate
cream doughnuts!
Follow the flashing lights!

I stumbled back through the snow as fast as I could.

"Look at the sign!" I called out as I put the boxes back in the trunk.

"Follow the flashing lights?" Jeanine said. "What is this? *The Wizard of Oz?*"

"Go, Dad, go!" I said as soon as I was back in the car.

By the time we reached the other end of Main Street, I knew where we were headed. The little station house exploded with so much light, you probably could have seen where we were headed from way out in space.

"Ooooooh! Pretty!" Zoe said.

Every inch of the little building flashed with tiny white lights that sparkled on the snow like a disco ball.

"It's a crime against the environment is what it is," Jeanine said.

"I don't believe it!" Mom said. "Do you see all those cars?"

"Where?" I said.

She put down her window and stuck her arm out. "Look!"

There, in the lot on the far side of the station house, sat mound after car- and truck-shaped mound of snow.

"They must have been here for hours," Dad said as he pulled up in front of the station house.

A hooded figure in an army-green parka climbed down the porch steps, waded through the snow to our car, and knocked on my window.

I put the window down, but before I had a chance to open my mouth, Jeanine pushed forward and stuck her head out. "Do you have any idea how much electricity you're wasting?"

Winnie rolled her eyes. "This the sister?"

"Yeah, one of them," I said.

"Do you even *know* we're in an energy crisis?" Jeanine went on.

"Yup," Winnie said.

"Jeanine," my father warned.

"Oh, don't stop her on my account. I can take it," Winnie said.

"So, don't you think we all have a responsibility to conserve electricity?" Jeanine said.

"I sure do," Winnie said.

"You do?" she said sadly. I could tell she'd been gearing up for a good fight.

"Yup. That's why I have all these lights on solar-powered batteries. Quite a project, but me and Dr. C got it done. Now if you don't mind, Slick's got to get in there and make me some money," she said, opening the car door. "Get going, Slick."

"I just have to get the doughnuts out of the back," I said as I got out.

"My condolences," Winnie said as we climbed the porch steps. "My brother Clive's a peach compared to that one."

"Camping blankets! Wool socks! Folding chairs! Beef jerky!" somebody called from inside the station house.

"What's that?"

"Harley. Gotta give the man credit. He certainly knows how to make the most of a business opportunity. I know it might seem like he was stealing your thunder, but look at it this way, if he hadn't brought in those portable heaters, no way people would have made it till now."

"Maybe I should thank him then."

"I wouldn't go that far. Let's just say it was mutually beneficial. He's made a killing on those folding chairs and wool socks. See for yourself," she said as she pushed open the door.

The place was packed, people everywhere, grown-ups, kids, some huddled around heaters, some sitting in circles of matching camping chairs, some lying on sleeping bags. Most I'd never seen before, but as I looked around, I spotted every person I'd met since coming to Petersville: Mr. Jennings from the turkey farm, Riley, Jim, Dr. Charney, Josh's mom, some families from the library, the kid from the Gas Mart.

And standing in the ticket window, opening the bag of napkins he'd brought from home just like he'd promised, was Josh. He smiled and waved.

"That kid's been up all night getting this place ready. Him and his mom and me and Jim and Dr. Charney, all of us," Winnie said. "We knew you'd be busy with the doughnuts. Place cleaned up pretty good, no?"

"Way better than pretty good," I said.

The garbage that had covered the floor had been replaced by overlapping rugs of all colors, shapes, and sizes. Red paper lanterns hung from the rafters, and colored lights wound around the little tree growing out of the middle of the floor.

But the biggest change since I'd peeked through the window on my first day in Petersville? A floor-to-ceiling steam engine painted in whites and grays like it was made of clouds stretched across the entire back wall.

"Did Dr. Charney do that?"

"When he wasn't helping with the lights. Paint isn't even dry," Winnie said.

"Where'd all these people come from?" I said, looking around the room.

"Where do you think? From here."

I guess it made sense that I didn't recognize most of them. Where would I have seen them? They couldn't have had any more of a clue who I was than I did who they were, but suddenly, the whole room was on its feet, clapping and cheering, closing in on me.

"Is that for Tris?" Zoe said, coming in behind me.

"Don't be silly, honey. It's for the doughnuts," Winnie said.

Just then, a man elbowed his way to the front of the crowd. From his yellow-white hair and matching teeth, I knew right away who he was.

"*You* back up," Winnie said, giving Clive a shove. "You get yours last."

"How come?" Clive said, frowning.

"Because. That's why," Winnie said, poking him in the gut.

"That's the thanks I get for printing you those nice stickers, free of charge?"

Winnie snorted. "Huh. Like that makes up for all the nonsense you put me through. Keep talking, and you don't get any."

"All right, all right. I'm going," Clive said and slunk back into the crowd.

"Hey, there, Mr. Doughnut Stop!" someone called. "Quite a turnout, huh?"

"Who was that?" I studied the crowd.

Winnie pointed to a corner of the room where Harley stood in front of a table piled high with surprisingly useful merchandise.

"Earmuffs?" He held up a pair with long, droopy dog ears.

"Nah, I'm good, thanks."

"C'mon, people, relax!" Winnie shooed everyone back. "We still got to get set up, so give us a little room here."

It took some work—and threats to revoke doughnut privileges—but eventually Winnie cleared a path for us from the front door to the ticket window.

"So, what do you think?" Josh said, popping up over the ticket counter. "I figured we could sell from inside the booth and then pass the doughnuts out through the window. Good idea?"

"Great idea!" I said.

"Did you see the sign?"

"Yeah, that's how I knew where to come."

"No, the other sign." He pointed up.

I put the doughnut boxes on the ticket counter and took a step back. Someone had hung Winnie's YES, WE DO HAVE CHOCOLATE CREAM DOUGHNUTS! sign on the wall above the window.

Winnie gave herself a pat. "My idea."

"Also your idea to set up here in the station house?" I said.

She laughed.

"What?"

"Jim told us it was yours," Josh said.

"Really?" Was this some other wink-wink with Jim the Mayor/Carpenter/Kidnapper that I wasn't in on? I scanned the room and spotted him standing by the back door, shovel in hand, talking to my mother. "Back in a sec."

"Still not checking those weather reports, huh, Jax?" Jim said when he saw me coming. "Tell me, what do you think of all this?"

"It's so cool, but why are you telling people it was my idea?"

"Because it was. Don't you remember what you told me that day? Town needs somewhere everybody can get together. You said this place was it."

I did remember. I just couldn't believe that he did, and that he'd thought it was such a good idea he'd just gone and done it.

"Look around. You were right." He turned me to face the room.

Zoe had joined a group of kids sitting on the floor listening to Riley play the guitar and was throwing in her own strum of the strings when she could sneak it in. Gonzo and Ziggy were there too, spread across the floor, being used as pillows. Dad was over by Harley's table talking with some people, and even from all the way across the room I knew which corny joke he was telling. At first, I didn't see Jeanine and wondered if maybe she was freezing in the car in protest, but then I spotted her in a corner, crouched over a chessboard opposite a man with a long, gray ponytail. Even though the man had racked up twice as many pieces as she had, for the first time in a very long time, she didn't look like she were wishing she were someplace else.

"Jim also told me you thought the station house would make a great restaurant. And you're so right," Mom said, smiling her biggest smile. "It's perfect! Even the name: the Station House. I love it. That's what we were just talking about. Putting my restaurant here. Since I wouldn't be serving breakfast, I'd be closed when the Doughnut Stop was open. You willing to share? You did see it first."

"I think we can work something out," I said.

"Very generous of you," Jim said, winking at me.

From across the room, Winnie waved me over. "Let's sell some doughnuts!" she called.

Jeanine jumped out of her chair and raced across the room to the ticket window. "Wait! Stop! I just had an idea. You guys should auction off the doughnuts."

"You mean sell them to the people who can pay the most?" Josh asked.

"Yeah. Think how much money you'll make. Look at these people. They're totally desperate."

"This girl reminds more of Clive every second," Winnie said.

"But then some people might not get any," Josh said.

"Yeah, but it's not as if you won't be selling them every week. They can get some next time. Come on. It's such a good idea."

I looked at Josh. He gave a little shrug like he wasn't sure, but I knew he was. He hated the idea, and so did I. How could we not give everyone a doughnut after they'd come out in the snow and waited all that time? These were loyal customers, and they deserved to be rewarded.

That's when I got my own idea.

"No auction, but we're not going to just sell either."

"We're not?" Josh said.

"What's the best way to create customer loyalty when you're starting a business?"

Josh grinned. "Free samples!"

"You're going to give them away?" Jeanine said. She looked disgusted.

"My doughnuts?" said Winnie, who looked just as disgusted. "For free?"

"We'll make money, just not today," I said. "It'll be good for business long term. I promise."

"I don't know," Winnie said.

"I know what I'm talking about, and I'm telling you, this is a smart business move. I'm thinking big picture. Trust me," I said.

"Oh, fine! Give them away. But I can't watch," Winnie said. Then she grabbed a doughnut, took a bite, and squeezed her eyes shut.

"So, how should we do this?" Josh said.

"Like this," I said and climbed up on the counter. "Come and get 'em!"

After everyone got a doughnut, we still had one left. I tried to give it to Jim, but he wouldn't take it. He said it would look bad for the mayor to get two doughnuts when everyone else had gotten only one. Jeanine agreed and told me that just by offering Jim the extra doughnut, I could be guilty of bribing a public official. Who knew? In the end, I gave the extra doughnut to Shane, the guy who'd beaten Jeanine at chess.

The party at the station house lasted way longer than the doughnuts did, so at lunchtime, Renny went down to the Gas Mart to pick up sandwich fixings. Unlike us though, he charged people for what they ate. Renny doesn't really think big picture, and I don't think he knows the first thing about creating customer loyalty.

We never regretted giving the doughnuts away that first day. It created so much buzz that the following week, we had twice as many people waiting for us when we showed up with the doughnuts even though they knew they'd have to pay this time.

That was three months ago, and business gets better every week. There's so much to do I've even given Zoe and Jeanine jobs. Winnie thought it was a huge mistake, but most of the time, Jeanine remembers she's not the boss, and when she forgets, I sic Winnie on her. Zoe doesn't make trouble because she knows if she does, she won't get paid, and she's saving up for a pastry gun of her own.

Since *Starting Your Own Business for Dummies* says your customers get bored if you don't offer different product lines, I've been experimenting with new cream flavors. None of the new flavors are life changing yet, but butterscotch and caramel are close.

You should come by sometime. I promise the Doughnut Stop's worth the trip. Just be sure to get there early. There's always a line, and we always sell out. Come when it snows, and the first one's free. Beat Jeanine at chess, and the second one's on the house too.

And, remember, ask for Jax, so I know who you are.

MOM'S MOLTEN CHOCOLATE CAKES

Makes 4 single-serve cakes

Ingredients

- 1 stick unsalted butter
- 6 ounces semisweet chocolate chips
- 2 egg yolks
- 2 eggs
- ¼ cup sugar
- 1 teaspoon vanilla extract
- 2 tablespoons all-purpose flour

Directions

1. Preheat the oven to 450°F.
2. Spray the insides of 4 ramekins with baking spray. Put the ramekins on a baking sheet.
3. Microwave the butter and chocolate chips in a microwave-safe bowl for 1 minute. The butter should be almost all melted. The chocolate won't be completely melted.
4. Whisk the butter and chocolate mixture until smooth.

5. Separate two egg yolks from their whites: Crack both eggs into a bowl without breaking the yolks. Then take an empty, disposable plastic water bottle, squeeze it, hold the opening to a yolk, and then release to suck the yolk into the bottle. Repeat with the second yolk. Then deposit both yolks into a clean bowl by squeezing the bottle and pouring them out.
6. Beat the egg yolks, eggs, sugar, and vanilla extract in an electric mixer on high or with a whisk until the mixture is thick.
7. Fold the butter and chocolate mixture into the egg mixture.
8. Add the flour to the mixture gradually. Don't overmix.
9. Divide the batter into the 4 ramekins.
10. Bake the cakes for 8 to 12 minutes or until the cakes have risen over the sides of the ramekins and the tops of the cakes no longer jiggle when the baking sheet is given a little shake. The cake centers should still be soft.
11. Remove the cakes from the oven and let them cool for 1 minute.
12. Cover the cakes with upside-down dessert plates, flip the ramekins over, and remove the ramekins from the cakes. Eat immediately!

PERFECT CHOCOLATE CHIP COOKIES

Makes 3 dozen cookies

Ingredients

1 cup light brown sugar

¼ cup granulated sugar

2 sticks unsalted butter, softened

2 eggs

1 teaspoon vanilla extract

1 teaspoon baking soda

1 pinch of salt

2 cups all-purpose flour

18 ounces semisweet chocolate, in bars

½ cup unsweetened shredded coconut

1 cup chopped walnuts

Directions

1. Preheat the oven to 350°F.
2. Cut parchment paper to cover baking sheets.
3. Put the light brown sugar, granulated sugar, and softened

butter into a large mixing bowl and cream together in an electric mixer on medium.

4. In a small bowl, crack the eggs and mix them with the vanilla extract.
5. Combine the egg mixture with the sugar and butter mixture and mix thoroughly on medium.
6. In another bowl, combine the baking soda, salt, and all-purpose flour.
7. Add the flour mixture to the sugar and butter mixture in the large bowl and mix on low. Don't overmix.
8. Break the chocolate bars into chunks.
9. Add the chocolate, coconut, and walnuts to the mixture and stir with a spoon.
10. Once combined, scoop the dough out with a tablespoon and place the balls on the baking sheet. Leave about two fingers width between each cookie.
11. Bake cookies for 12 minutes.
12. Remove cookies from the oven and leave on the baking sheet for 1 minute. Then, transfer the cookies to a wire rack to cool.

ROOKIE CINNAMON SUGAR DOUGHNUTS*

Parental supervision necessary for frying

Makes 8 doughnuts and 8 doughnut holes

Ingredients

Vegetable oil

1 (8-count) tube of premade, large biscuit dough (found in the refrigerated dough aisle at supermarkets)

½ cup sugar

¼ teaspoon ground cinnamon

Directions

1. Fill a large saucepan with vegetable oil to a depth of 1 inch.
2. Heat oil over medium heat until it reaches 365°F. You can measure the temperature with a cooking oil thermometer. Or, drop a single kernel of popcorn into the oil as it's heating. When the kernel pops, you're ready to fry.
3. While the oil heats, open the biscuit tube and separate the

rounds. Use a 1-inch-round cookie cutter to cut a hole in the center of each biscuit. Save the holes.

4. Mix the sugar and cinnamon in a large shallow bowl.
5. Add 2 doughnuts to the hot oil at a time. Cook, turning once, until golden brown—about 1 minute per side.
6. Drain on paper towels and immediately toss in the cinnamon sugar to coat. Cool on a wire rack. Repeat with the remaining doughnuts and holes.

* Ready to graduate from rookie to experienced baker? You can make the Doughnut Stop's life-changing chocolate cream doughnuts too. Visit jessiejanowitz.com for the original recipe.

THE CHEAT SHEET

(No, that doesn't mean you're a cheater! It means you're smart enough to read past the last page, so you get a recap of important information for starting your own business.)

The Secret: Find Your Thing

Okay, you've got a business idea. Great. Here's what you need to ask before you get started:

- **Do I know anything about this?**
- **If not, keep looking.**

Hint: What do you like to do? Eat chocolate? Skateboard? Draw bunny cartoons? That's where *your* business idea is.

The Lingo (a.k.a. Fancy Words You Need to Know)

No, you can't skip this part, or people will rip you off and your business will fail before you even start. Is that what you want? Yeah, didn't think so.

Business Plan

an explanation of what your business is, how it works, and why it will be a hit

Hint: If you're having trouble with this, you're not starting the right business. Go back and find *your* thing.

Hook

the thing that makes your product especially cool

Still don't get what a hook is? Some examples:

Our shoes are made from recycled milk cartons—cool!
Our pencil cases turn into rain jackets—cool!
Our Popsicles make you nicer—huh? But still, cool!

If you don't have a hook, you're in trouble. Oh, and if you can't explain the hook in one sentence, it's not really a hook.

Revenue

money you get from selling your product

Be realistic. People won't spend a million dollars on a bunny cartoon even if it is really cute and funny.

Costs

the money you spend to run your business

Costs include stuff like what you spend to make your product or pay your workers or rent your store/office.

Profit

the money you make from your business

Don't confuse this with revenue. Profit is the money you get from customers minus all the money you have to pay to keep your business going.

Actually important math you will need to figure out your profit:

Subtract your costs from your revenue.

$ Profits = $ Revenue – $ Costs

Budget

what you guess your revenue, costs, and profits will be

Hint: You can't just make this up. You have to do research to figure out what your costs are actually going to be and how much people will actually pay for whatever it is you're selling.

Contract

an agreement

When you make a deal with anyone, get what you and the other person are agreeing to **in writing** *and make sure you both sign it.*

Negotiate

to talk your way to a better deal

This takes practice, but it's worth it. And, no, you can't get arrested for negotiating, though people may yell at you.

Hint: Never take anyone's first offer.

Investors

people who lend you money to start your business and share in the profits

Hint: People don't invest to be nice even if they're related to you. They will invest if they believe in your product, and they see that you believe in it too. They can't get excited about your business unless you are.

Buzz

when people get so excited about your product that they talk it up all over town and on the internet

The Game Plan: Now What?

Once you've got the lingo down, make a road map, something like:

- **Step 1: Come up with a business plan and hook.**

- **Step 2: Figure out a budget.**

- **Step 3: Make sure your product does what it's supposed to. (It can't just be a cool idea; it has to work.)**

- **Step 4: Pitch investors.**

- **Step 5: Negotiate and make deals with investors and people you will need to buy things from to make your product.**

- **Step 6: Create buzz.**

- **Step 7: Launch business!**

Then give each step a deadline so you won't look up in a year and realize you never got past Step 1. Timelines have also been shown to prevent people from chickening out.

The Starting Line: 3, 2, 1...Start Your Business!

Go!

What are you still doing here? You know where to come if you need a quick refresher, but right now, you need to go find your thing, and that's all *you,* so get going!

ACKNOWLEDGMENTS

Writing a book is not so different from making pudding: you stir and stir and wonder whether your story will actually come together before your arm falls off. I am so grateful to everyone who gave me the tools and the encouragement to keep stirring:

My mother especially, who first taught me how, writing down my stories before I could write them myself, though their plots bore a striking similarity to that of *Star Wars*.

The women who so generously read drafts of this book and offered feedback: Rebecca Sokolovsky, Amy Fontaine, Noël Claro, Dagmar Gleditzsch, Rebecca Kirshenbaum, and Randall de Sève.

The Rutgers Council on Children's Literature and the Society of Children's Book Writers and Illustrators for giving me the tools to send my pudding out into the world.

My incredible friends at Vermont College of Fine Arts for supporting me, and the amazing faculty for focusing me on what's important and sharing inspiring stirring advice.

My agent, Carrie Hannigan, and her assistant, Tanusri Prasanna, at the Hannigan Salky Getzler Agency for falling in love with these characters and believing that others would too.

My editor Annie Berger for wanting to bring this story to young readers. This book is so much stronger because of her guidance. A huge thank-you also to everyone else at Sourcebooks who worked on this project, especially Elizabeth Boyer, production editor; Nicole Hower, cover designer; as well as Nina Goffi, cover illustrator. I couldn't be happier.

My smart, talented, loving friends because stirring would be impossible without knowing they have my back. Without naming names, please forgive me for borrowing Tawatty Tawatty Dabu Dabu.

My father for always believing I could conquer anything I set my mind to.

My brother, Will, who I can always talk to about the painful stirring and know he'll get it, for his constant support.

And finally, the home team—Toby, who was the first to say I was good enough; Leo, who first called me an author; Sylvie, who always, always believes; and Eddie, who asked, "Are you doing what makes you happy?"—none of this is possible without you.